Jess

Pauline George

Yellow Rose Books
by Regal Crest

Texas

ISBN 978-1-61929-138-6

First Printing 2014

9 8 7 6 5 4 3 2 1

Original cover design by Donna Pawlowski
Final cover design by AcornGraphics

Published by:

Regal Crest Enterprises, LLC
229 Sheridan Loop
Belton, TX 76513

Find us on the World Wide Web at
http://www.regalcrest.biz

Printed in the United States of America

Acknowledgments

I would like to thank Cathy Byerose who had faith in me. All the team at Regal Crest: AcornGraphics for the great cover, Verda for making the editing process so easy — *Jess* is all the better for your work — and Patty for putting up with all my silly questions.

Special thanks go to Helen — the best sister in the world, Sue, Lisa, Julie and Bev for reading and helping me get *Jess* ready for going out into the big wide world. My Mum and Dad — who isn't around to see my success — both of them gave me my love of reading, their love and support.

Thanks also to Joy Swift MBE of Joy Swift's Original Murder Weekends for allowing me use her name and the description of one of her plots in Jess.

To G this much times a million.

Chapter One

HI, MY NAME is Jess. God, it sounds as if I'm at an AA meeting — not that I've ever been to an AA meeting — don't get me wrong, I've nothing against AA meetings. I guess they do a good job. I mean, I don't really know, as I said I've never been to one.

But, hey, I digress.

What I really wanted was to introduce myself to you. This is my story, if you're interested. Well, I think it's interesting, but then I would. I mean, I'm actually living it and it seems pretty good to me. So, I guess you want to know a bit about me and where I live? Well, I work in public transport and have a fantastic job as a signal operator. Oh, great, I hear you say. Yes, it's just like playing with a giant train set and so much fun. I live in Croydon which, for the uninitiated, is just outside London. I live across the road from a lovely park where I go for walks in the sun, when we get some. Don't you just love the great English weather? I'm lucky enough to have my own house, but not so lucky in the way I got it. Our parents died in a road accident and left the house to me and Josie. Because Josie already had her own house with her partner Ivan, I bought her out and now it belongs to me. Well, me and the mortgage company. I like to play the field a little, okay a lot, but what is life if it's not for living? Although Josie wouldn't agree, she reckons my life is quite sad.

"Jess, I really think you should settle down. You don't look happy."

She thinks my life's sad because I haven't settled down. Oh boy.

"Okay, Josie. Why do you think I look unhappy?"

Josie thought for a moment. I swear I could see all the little cogs inside her head working away. We were sitting in my kitchen at the big pine table just chilling, I thought, enjoying each other's company. The kitchen is my favourite room. It's not as big as the one in Mel's place, but it's okay. I can only seat four of us at the table so when there's a crowd we go into the dining room. I decorated the walls in a warm sunshine yellow with a white ceiling, doors and surrounds. My units are pine with black granite work surfaces and a butler sink. At one end of the kitchen are large double doors leading out to the garden and I love to open them whenever I can, to let the garden in so to speak. My next project is to put a patio outside so I can eat alfresco and have a few barbecues. The table sits right by the door, so when it's open I feel like I'm in the garden as well as the kitchen. Josie comes round a lot and has her own key. I sometimes wonder if that was a mistake on my part. Only kidding, I love my little sister, even when she likes to have a go at me, which she is about to do.

"Well you're not with anyone," she said, with no real conviction.

My wonderful sister — well she is sometimes — thinks that to be happy you have to be with someone.

"In fact, you're never really with anyone."

She fooled me. She had given this a lot of thought. Boy, did that one sting.

"Okay, not at the moment, but I'm sure it won't last."

I think I'm what they call a serial monogamist. Yes, honestly. I'm only with one person at a time. The trouble is, that time is never very long. I usually last a couple of weeks then move on to the next one. At this rate, there'll be no lesbians left I haven't had a relationship with. Mind you, you can hardly call a couple of weeks anything more than a fling. Perhaps there's something wrong with me if I can't make a relationship last more than that.

"So, Oracle Sister of mine, what's wrong with me?"

Not sure I really meant to say that out loud. Oh shit, too late. Josie's thought process was starting up and there would be no stopping it now.

"Well, first off, stop being so sarcastic."

Was that it? If I stop being sarky all my troubles will be cured? I must have looked smug — I do that occasionally — because she gave me her very best stare. Boy was I in trouble now.

"No, it won't cure all your troubles."

I could hear the pain in her voice. Just how did she know what I was thinking?

"All I'm saying is stop being sarky to me. I don't deserve it."

"Yeah, you're right. I'm sorry, I didn't mean it." I gave her my best I'm really, really sorry look.

"And don't think you can get away with it by doing your — I'm so sorry — look on me."

Josie is obviously not impressed with me at the moment. But she's my little sister. She loves me really.

"Look, what I'm saying is that you don't give yourself time for a break in between relationships."

I got up to put the kettle on. I needed time to think about what she'd said. Some conversations have to be had with copious amounts of tea, and I could tell this was going to be one of those. While I made the tea I tried to think about my situation and how I'd got in this not so good place. I poured two mugs of tea, put them on the table, and got the biscuits. You can't have tea without dunking a dozen or so.

"Look, Sis, I'm never with anyone long enough to worry about having a break in between."

I dunked my biscuit and popped it into my mouth. No, not the whole thing, I'm not a complete moron. I just broke a mouth sized piece off and dunked it. I can be quite genteel when I want.

"Yeah, well, maybe that's the problem. Ever since that bitch, Sue, you haven't been able to go the distance with anyone."

"It's got nothing to do with Sue. That was finished over a year ago now."

"Oh, don't give me that crap," she said. "You know very well you've not been able to trust anyone since her."

Josie was really on one now. She had her counselling hat on and the session was about to begin.

"Don't forget, I was there picking up the pieces she scattered to the four winds."

"Yeah, I know, and I'm really grateful. But I'm over her now."

"I wish I could believe you. I think you need to find someone really special who'll be good to you, treat you as an equal. Not like a little puppy dog."

Josie could really hit the nail on the head and it usually felt like mine.

"Sue would say jump and you'd ask, how high?"

"And where am I going to find that special someone?" I asked in my best sarcastic voice, which I immediately knew was a big mistake. I tried to retrieve the situation. "Sorry, Josie, I didn't mean to say it like that."

"Okay, I'll let you off this time."

That was a close call.

"You need to get out and meet women to talk to. Get to know them first, not jump into bed the minute you've set eyes on them."

She was right as usual. I did jump into bed quicker than you could say sex, but I wasn't going to let her know how right she was.

"Of course I can be with someone without jumping into bed on the first date." I hoped I sounded more convincing than I actually felt.

Mind you, I've had more than my fair share of sexual encounters. Thinking about it though, most of them left me feeling empty and wanting more. Not more sex, you understand, although that would be really great. No, what I mean is, I was usually satisfied, yes. Thinking about it now I was, sort of. But I always felt empty afterwards, like there was something missing. I guess it was the kind of thing Sue and I'd had. We'd had a relationship, sex, love, companionship and friendship. She was my best friend, my lover. She was also a liar and a cheat, but hey, her loss. Still, at least I know I'm capable of having a meaningful relationship and that it lasted four years. Not bad eh?

I must have said that last bit out loud, because my little sister decided to give me her take on it.

"Look Jess, you and Sue were good together, while it was good."

Wow, my sister sure can be incisive.

"But—"

Yes, there had to be a but.

"She really fucked with your head. You just don't have the confidence to go into another long-term relationship. You think you deserve to be treated badly and when you're not, you don't know how to handle it."

Josie could really get to the crux of it.

"I can have a long meaningful relationship if I want," I said a little petulantly, but trying to sound confident.

"Yes you can, I know that, but will you? Personally, I don't think you can go out with someone without jumping their bones first and ruining the possibility of more."

I heard the sadness for me in her voice. That kind of put my back up, it was a challenge. Little sis had thrown down the gauntlet. Did I have the courage to pick it up? Yes. I would prove her wrong. I would do it.

"Of course I can."

"All right then prove it. The next woman you fancy you've got to woo her."

"Oh I say old bean, I have to woo her," I said, in a mock posh accent.

"Yeah okay, I didn't mean it quite like that. I just mean you should get to know her before you jump her bones, but she's not allowed to know what's going on. This is just between us."

"God, Josie, you really know how to pile on the pressure."

I was banking on the fact that I could let this woman know, get her to go along with it so I could prove Josie wrong. Yes, I know it's devious. But don't you think Josie's being devious too? No? Okay, I guess you're right. She's just looking out for me. What she doesn't know is I fancy two of her mates. At least I could go out with them and not jump straight into bed, although I'm sure they're curious. However, I'm not into the experiment, straight women who want to try it out, just to see what it's like. Mind you, Katie's really hot and I would gladly experiment with her any day and all day long. Ah, well, I can dream can't I?

"Okay, you're on. The next time I see a really hot woman, I'll take it very slowly and see how it goes."

I made a decision that I'd give it a go. I've been on my own too long, feeling sorrier for myself than I would admit to anyone. I mean, how hard can it be to abstain from sex? A friend of mine went three years without sex. Well, two person sex. She was Duracell's best customer. I'd have a hard time lasting three days. But that was going to have to change. Josie was right, I couldn't treat women in the cavalier fashion I had been if I wanted a chance at happiness. I needed to be more responsible. Big word I know, but I should treat women with respect, which also meant having more respect for myself. I had to be less shallow. As it stood now, a puddle had more depth than me.

"So how are we gonna fix me up? I'm sure Katie and Shelley would be up for it." I so loved teasing Josie.

"Forbidden territory. I know you fancy Katie, but she's off limits and she's married."

How did she know I fancied Katie? I swear she's a mind reader. Still she took it all in good part.

"Yeah, but—"

"No, Jess, leave Katie alone. I'm serious."

"It's all right, the only thing I'll be doing with Katie, is giving her a friendly hug when she's down. You know me, the ever willing shoulder to cry on."

"Sorry for getting heavy, but you know she's having marital problems at the moment."

"I'm not surprised with that husband of hers."

"So let's leave Katie out of it then. There are plenty of other women for you to choose from."

Now I'm for it. I've taken up Josie's challenge and I can't back down. I mean I really don't want to prove my little sister right. She's nearly always right and that pisses me off. Actually, to be fair, it's more the fact that I'm wrong than she's right that pisses me off. I'm supposed to be wiser and the one who's always right. I've earned it, I'm the oldest. Trouble is Josie's twenty-five going on forty, whereas I'm twenty-eight going on twelve. She had to grow up quickly when our parents died. I just went to pieces while she kept it and me together. Now she's really got her life sorted. She knows where she's going and what she's going to do when she gets there.

She's got Ivan, her partner, a great fella who absolutely adores her. What wouldn't I give to have a female version of him? Still, I'm very lucky in that she's embraced my sexuality and my friends, hence the fact that we all go out together on many occasions. Josie's friends are great. I get on with them really well, especially as they take my flirting all in good fun. Katie, Shelley and Lou, Josie's best friends, really enjoy gay pubbing and clubbing. I think it's because they know there won't be any guys hitting on them. Yes, I know what you're going to say, what about the girls hitting on them? Well, I told them to say, "Thanks for asking and I'm very flattered, but I'm straight." It's much nicer than telling them to fuck off and it saves any bad feeling. My mates, Mel, Lisa and Lori, are used to the straight girlies, as they call them, and love to tease them. We have such a laugh when we're at Nexus, our local gay club. Whenever there's a slow dance, we pair off gay and straight, as if we're starring in *Dancing with the Stars*. It's great fun and gives everyone else a laugh. Most of the regulars at Nexus are used to our crowd and we all have a wicked time. Trouble is I'm sure there's a bit of Josie that thinks I'm seriously trying to get off with her mates. She likes to give me the evil eye occasionally, just like a friendly shot across the bow. I keep telling her that it's just a bit of fun, but I guess she remembers that night at Nexus when I started to fancy Katie. I hoped she hadn't noticed, yes all right I'm getting to it, I know you're curious.

Well a few months ago...

"WHO'S UP FOR Nexus on Saturday?" I asked the gang in the pub. We were all there for our regular mid-week session, me, Josie, Mel, Lou, Shelley, Lori, Katie and Lisa.

"Sounds great," Katie replied.

"Yeah, count me in too," Lou said.

"All right hands up who doesn't want to go," I said, there was no response.

"Great, let's meet here about eight thirty for a couple of drinks and hit the club about ten."

A general murmur of agreement followed.

We never went to the club earlier than ten. If you got there before that it was empty and no talent, but after and it was so full you couldn't get one of the good spots, which was just on the outside of the action, but where you could still watch it all. There were a couple of leather sofas and a few tables and we usually tried to grab one of those. The girlies had to have somewhere for their handbags, and I don't mean just the straight girlies. Me, I just put all I need into my jeans pockets and I'm away. I don't have make-up and stuff like that to worry about.

Okay, okay, I guess you want to know what I look like. Well, I'm no oil painting as they say, but I guess I'm passable. This is what Josie has to say on the matter, "you have a nice open face, full sensuous kissable lips—the lips bit was what one of her friends said, but she won't say which one—short spiky blonde hair, too short for my liking, reasonable figure, curvy not skinny." Okay, here's the official version. I'm five foot seven tall, with a fulle curvy figure. I could do with losing a few pounds but I'm lazy and love my food. Yes, my hair is short, but it's great for me, despite what Josie said. I'm not one for doing the blow-dry thing when I go out now I've found a style to suit me. It's great. The blonde is out of a bottle and I like it best when the roots show as it gives it a nice two-tone effect. So who do I look like that you guys might recognise? Think of Kylie, no just kidding, I'm nothing like her. Actually I look more like Shane from The L Word with blonde hair. And I guess I'm like her in character at the moment. You know, love 'em and leave 'em. Yes, I know, that's got to change. Also I'm not as skinny as Shane, definitely not as skinny, wish I was. I like that whole slim boyish look, at least on me. I like my women to have a bit of meat on them.

What about Josie, I hear you ask? Well, we're as different as chalk and cheese. She's quite a bit shorter than me at five foot two but what she lacks in height she makes up by being really confident and assertive. Josie is my rock, the one steadying influence in my life since Mum and Dad died. Josie's very feminine and has really good dress sense. Instead of jeans she'll nearly always wear a pair of tailored trousers. I think she's got some jeans but I've only seen her in them a few times. Josie's a natural beauty needing the barest amount of makeup and her shoulder length hair is a lovely, thick rich auburn.

Chapter Two

WE ALL MET up on Saturday as arranged and sat chatting in the pub until we went on to Nexus. Josie and her girlies looked great as usual, nice short skirts, which all of us gay girlies just loved. I'm sure they did it on purpose, not that I'm complaining you understand. Anyway, I realised that Katie and I had sort of split from the rest and were having our own conversation. The others were having a discussion about what to do for Mel's up-coming birthday. I decided to let them get on with it and concentrate on what Katie was saying. She was talking about kids. I prefer babies until they get to about three or four, after that I'm not so keen. There's that whole thing about being responsible for another human being. Hell, I'm hardly responsible for myself, let alone another little person who will be totally dependent on me for God only knows how many years.

"Bill really wants us to start a family but I don't know if I want to yet," Katie said. "And now he's blaming me for not getting pregnant."

"God, men are so unfair," I said angrily. "They blame us women for not being able to conceive when it might just be the fact that they're firing blanks."

"Right, now he wants me to see the doctor to get it sorted out. I'm not sure I want to go." Katie took a long swig of her lager and sat looking into space.

"I suppose the question you have to ask yourself is, do you really want to have kids or not?"

"That's the problem. I'm not sure and that's no way to bring another life into the world, is it? Any child I have has got to be wanted, by the both of us." Katie paused. "Oh I don't know — I just don't know what I want anymore. I'm so confused."

My heart went out to Katie. She seemed totally miserable with the situation she was in.

"Look, Katie, why don't you have a long chat with Bill and tell him how you feel? I'm sure he'll understand."

I felt sure Bill wouldn't understand at all. He was one of those men who wanted the little woman at home, with his dinner ready on the table when he returned from work. If he had his way he'd stop her from going out altogether. It took Katie a long time to persuade him she should continue to work after they got married. My thoughts on it are that he only wants to start a family so he has a reason to stop her working, thus getting his own way. Katie's husband wasn't the nicest of men. He never hit her or anything like that, he just wasn't very nice. His was emotional abuse. He enjoyed putting her down in front of her mates, especially now they were trying for kids and not having much luck. It would appear from what Katie said, he was making it out to be all her fault. But he conveniently forgot they'd only been trying for a couple of months.

"I love kids, but I couldn't eat a whole one." I was hoping to lighten the mood as Katie was becoming sad and withdrawn.

I looked at her for a moment and thought she was going to hit me. Then a large grin spread over her face and she laughed out loud. The others turned to see what the joke was and I just shrugged.

"Thanks, Jess, you know just when to say the right thing. I was going off on one then and we're supposed to be having fun."

I was so glad she took it the right way. I could have had a nasty black eye otherwise. She touched me lightly on the arm. I felt the heat of her fingers on my skin. I caught her eyes and held them just a little longer than I maybe should have. But then Katie didn't break away either. I could've sworn she was checking me out. I felt my skin tingle and my stomach clench as a spasm of arousal coursed through me. Jesus.

"No, er — it's all right. You weren't going off on one at all." I broke eye contact to pick up my drink. I needed to focus again and not think about what had just passed between us. "You were just feeling down and sharing it and that's okay if it makes you feel better. Now let's go and have some fun."

Just as I said that, Mel shouted that we should make a move or miss getting a good table. We drank up and left the pub for the short walk to Nexus, which is great on a nice warm summer evening. Only Josie, Mel and Shelley joined me, the rest jumped on the very convenient bus at the very convenient bus stop outside the pub. Lazy buggers. Shelley and Mel went off together leaving my little sis, who linked arms with me.

"What were you and Katie talking about?"

God, Josie is so protective of Katie. I had no idea why.

"Babies," I said curtly, "just what is it with you and Katie?"

"I've known her since we were at school together and I suppose I regard her as my best, best friend. There's a lot of stuff going on with her that I can't tell you."

"I get that but why are you so keen to stop me talking to her?"

"I'm not stopping you talking to her, I was just curious," Josie said gently. "She's going through a rough time. I wondered if she'd said anything to you that might shed light on why she's down at the moment."

"Okay, sorry. I just thought you were protecting her from your big bad dyke sister." I turned to look at her hoping she'd appreciated the joke.

"Of course not. I know you better than that." Josie sounded hurt that I thought she would even think like that.

"Sorry, Josie I didn't mean to be flip. You know me. I joke about fancying your mates, but I'm not serious. Even though they're good looking, it doesn't mean I want to jump their bones."

"I know that Jess and I'm sorry. I didn't mean to come on with the heavy hand about Katie."

"Okay, no worries. Let's just go and have some fun, eh?" I squeezed her hand and gave her my best cheesy grin.

"Yeah let's have a really great night, I feel like getting pissed," she shouted as we neared the club.

The others turned and looked at her in amazement. Josie never has more than a couple of drinks. Sometimes my sister is too nice for her own good. She takes on the world's problems and tries to sort them all out. Trouble is, when she can't sort them, as with Katie, she gets down. I guess this was one of those times I'd just have to keep an eye on her. I didn't want her going silly and getting really drunk. She's only done it once and she was very ill. I know that feeling and it's awful. Not that it stops me getting off my head every now and again, but not Josie, she's much too sensible.

I needn't have worried as the first drink Josie ordered was a Diet Coke. But even on Diet Coke she can really enjoy herself. My sister doesn't need alcohol or drugs, she's high on life.

The DJs were playing a great mix of music, but it was a while before they slowed it down. I think we'd been up dancing the whole time and were glad of the drop in pace. As usual we all did our Fred and Ginger routine, assuming the formal dancing positions. I seemed to be the odd one out with no partner and was about to leave the dance floor when a hand slipped into mine. I felt a tingle, like an electric shock, and turned to see who it was. I was hoping for some gorgeous dyke who wanted to dance with me. But no, it was Katie. And yes, she is drop dead gorgeous and I wanted nothing more than to get my arms around her, but she was not the gorgeous dyke I was hoping for. Anyway she was off-limits, wasn't she?

"May I have the pleasure of this dance?" she asked with a grin on her face.

"Why, of course you may." I held out my arms to take the lead as she moved into my arms and we started to dance.

"Do you come here often?" she asked, hardly able to suppress a giggle.

"Actually I do, how about you?"

"Thanks for earlier," she said. "I needed to talk. I'm just sorry about the timing."

"Don't worry about it. I was glad to help."

Was it my imagination, or did Katie move her body closer to mine? Not that I'm complaining you understand. Definitely not complaining. She has a very hot body and could hold it against me all night. I felt her nipples harden, which sent my blood rapidly south. Here is where I had to remind myself that she's straight, married and about to start a family, blah, blah. But her perfume was intoxicating. It was reaching the parts other perfumes couldn't and I was getting very hard and wet. Yes, I could have pulled away, but I was enjoying myself way too much. And, it might be the only time I would ever have the chance to be this close to the woman of my dreams. Oh okay, my lust! Although to be honest it was more than that, much more but—

"You're a really nice person, Jess. Any woman would be mad not to go out with you." She moved in closer again. No, I didn't imagine it and I was having a hard time keeping control of myself.

She sounded a little drunk, maybe that's why she was being so bold.

"I just wish I could find a woman. Do you know any?" I tried to make a joke, but her closeness was really beginning to get to me.

My centre throbbed, I was becoming so aroused. This should not be happening. I was cruising for a bruising as there was no way Katie and I were ever going to bed with each other. But she was really testing my resolve about not getting involved with a straight woman. I so wanted to kiss her, caress her, and feel her soft skin beneath my fingers. I was in so much trouble.

"I may." She moved closer and rested her head against me.

I looked round to see if anyone could see us. Fortunately, the others were busy chatting while they danced. I must admit to holding her close when she moved in the last time. It felt so good. We fit together so perfectly, as they say in all the romances. So why was it wrong? I really wished at that moment there was a gay fairy, sorry about the pun, who would put a spell on Katie. The music changed to a fast dance and Katie pulled away and looked up at me. Time seemed to stand still. God, that look, it hit me in the pit of my stomach, like an iron fist, and left me breathless.

Have you seen *Notting Hill*? The bit when Julia gets into the garden. Poor old Hugh only just makes it without lancing his balls on the railings. She looks at him like that just before she kisses him. Gets me every time. Katie's look was exactly the same and her hazel eyes held mine for what seemed like forever. I was drowning in a pool of soft, melted chocolate. I couldn't look away. My clitoris twitched as wetness pooled between my legs. I was losing myself out there on the dance floor. She moved closer, her lips parting, ready to kiss me and God help me, I was moving in too.

Then I caught sight of Josie out of the corner of my eye heading toward us. God I had to be quick. I kissed Katie on the cheek and bowed to her.

"Thank you kind madam for the dance. I shall now away to the bar for another round of drinks."

If looks could kill, the one Josie threw my way would have put me six foot under. She grabbed my arm and took me to the ladies. All dyke drama and dyke sex happens in the ladies. Trust me, it's a bugger when you actually need to go to the toilet.

"What the hell was that all about with you and Katie on the dance floor?"

She went straight for the jugular.

"You would've kissed her if you hadn't seen me coming, wouldn't you?"

She was really mad. Not that I could blame her. She was right. I would have kissed Katie. But then she was about to kiss me and I was not about to pass up that opportunity.

"Now look, before you get all high and mighty, she came on to me. Don't look at me like that, I'm telling the truth. Yes, I would have kissed her, but only because she was about to kiss me, so why am I getting all the blame? I don't know what came over her. She's a bit miserable and a bit drunk. Perhaps because I took the time to listen to her she felt grateful. I don't know and I'm really confused about the whole thing."

I turned away from Josie, ending the confrontation and walked out of the ladies. I went back to the table to get my drink, which I could really do with now. All of us in the group know we don't overstep the mark and Katie had done that. It wasn't fair I was feeling something I didn't want to feel. Well, at least not for a straight woman. I was angry that Josie thought what had happened on the dance floor, or not happened, in this case, was all my doing. She saw, she formed an opinion and she came to have a go at me.

I flopped down on a chair next to Mel and took a long swig of my lager.

"Are you okay, Jess?" she asked looking at me, concern written all over her face. Mel's a counsellor and a bloody good one at that. She works mostly with young women having trouble coming to terms with their sexuality. A lot of her clients have problems with their families so she'll work with them as well, if they agree to it. She's great at what she does and can recognise when one of us is in trouble and always tries to help.

"No, not really, but I don't want to talk about it now," I said.

"Okay my place, eleven tomorrow. We'll have time for a chat

before the others come over for dinner."

I'd forgotten it was the first Sunday in the month tomorrow. This was when Lori, Lou and I went round to Mel's for one of her legendary roasts. My mouth started to salivate at the thought of it.

"That would be great. I could do with a chat. Thanks, Mel." I finished my lager and went to the bar to get another round in.

Katie and Josie had their heads together chatting away. I wished I could be a fly on the wall. I wondered if Josie was asking Katie if I'd come on to her. I wasn't worried, really I wasn't. I'd done nothing wrong. I knew where the line was and I wasn't the one who overstepped it. Katie had and I wanted to know why. I know I'm a good catch. No, seriously, I am and I always give good value when I take a woman out. That aside, why did she behave the way she had? Maybe she wanted to kiss a woman to see what it would be like. That's fine, I'm quite happy to oblige as long as I know that's what it is. But a big no-no is going with a straight woman. It only leads to heartache in the end. I know I really like Katie, okay then fancy the pants off her, but nothing could happen. It would be so easy to fall for her and make a complete fool of myself.

I took the drinks back to the table, still curious about what Katie and Josie were talking about.

The evening had suddenly lost its appeal for me and I really wanted to get out of there. Being a shift worker, I can cry off with tiredness and no one thinks much about it. So that's what I did, I just had to get away.

I decided to walk home. I'm one of the rare ones in our little group who actually likes to walk. It was a beautiful clear night and my way home was brightly lit, so I had no worries about walking this late. I hadn't gone more than a hundred yards when a car pulled up.

"Hi, Jess, want a lift home?" It was Scott from work.

"I was gonna walk, but seeing as how you're offering, yeah, that'd be nice, ta." I got in the car quite glad of the lift. It would give me more time at home to think about what happened at Nexus.

"You're going home early, aren't you?" Scott asked as he pulled away into the traffic.

"Yeah, I'm not feeling so bright tonight. Working shifts takes it out of you now and again. I just fancied going home early to get my beauty sleep."

I tried to be jolly with Scott, but I really didn't want to talk. I just wanted to get home.

"I know what you mean. I've just finished and I'm absolutely knackered."

Fortunately Scott wasn't up for chatting and the rest of the journey was silent. He pulled up outside my house.

"There you go, Jess. Sorry about the lack of conversation."

"No worries, Scott, I'm not feeling chatty myself. See you next week, I'm off tomorrow."

"Lucky you. I'm not off for a couple of days yet."

Scott drove off and I went indoors.

When I'm at home I love to doss about in old sweats and T-shirts. I call them scuzzies. Right now I really needed the comfort of my scuzzies. I went upstairs and found some sweats and a paint-spattered T-shirt. Then back downstairs and poured an ice-cold lager. I went into the lounge, found a nice soothing piece of music and sat thinking. I re-ran the evening through in my head — several times. I knew I'd done nothing to encourage Katie to behave the way she did. Not that I'm complaining. I mean, if I never get looked at like that again, God it was a look to die for. And her smile always gets to me.

I guess it's confession time.

Yes, I know I should have mentioned it earlier.

Ever since I met Katie about a year ago...

"Jess, we're over here."

My sister's voice rang out above the noise. We'd arranged to meet at 'The Bird', my local gay pub. Josie and her mates love it there, much as they do at Nexus.

I looked over and saw Josie sitting with a really attractive woman I'd not seen before. As I got closer, I thought her face seemed vaguely familiar. God was I hoping I hadn't made a fool of myself somewhere along the line.

Josie got up to give me a hug and a kiss and then turned to the mystery woman.

"Jess, this is Katie. You remember, my best friend from school?"

I looked again. Now I remembered. She was pretty in school but now she was absolutely gorgeous. I smiled my best ever smile. It never failed.

"Yes, I remember. Hi, Katie, how are you?"

Where have you been all my life?

She got up and we shook hands. I'd have preferred a hug and kiss from her and to shake hands with my sister, rather than the other way around.

Katie smiled back at me. "Fine thanks, how are you?"

What a smile. It was a knockout. I'd obviously not made a fool of myself because I would have remembered Katie, and I certainly wouldn't have let her get away.

"I'm great. What have you been up to then?"

I was curious to know where she'd been all this time. Why hadn't I seen her on the scene and how come I didn't know Josie had a gay friend? You couldn't have missed her. She was about the same height as me, but slimmer with great tits. Sorry, that was a bit laddish, as an old work colleague used to say. But she did have a great cleavage and I had to be careful not to stare. Well at least not get caught doing it. But then, she's in a gay pub, what does she expect? She was wearing a low-cut tight fitting vest top and a pair of tight cropped Capri pants with ballet shoes. How could I not look? Her hair was a rich auburn with copper highlights and cut so it just fell about her shoulders. It looked so soft and silky I had to resist reaching out and putting a stray bit of hair behind her ear. She had the loveliest hazel eyes, and they seemed to look right into me. I just hoped she couldn't read my thoughts.

"When Josie and I left school, my parents emigrated to Australia and I went with them, but I never planned to stay out there forever. I came back about six months ago. I actually met my husband out there. He's English and was on a working holiday," Katie said.

Oh, so it was that Katie. Everything came back to me now. The airmail letters and, of late, emails from Australia. Mind you, once there was the mention of a husband I had a job keeping my disappointment at bay. Of course I'd noticed the rings on the third finger of the left hand. I just didn't see them, if you know what I mean.

So, I do have a bit of a history with Katie, although not the kind of history I wanted. I guess if I'm honest with myself, I've fancied her since that meeting. Now can you understand my confusion at her behaviour on the dance floor? Why did she look at me like that? Why did she almost kiss me? I know we'd done a bit of bonding with our chat in the pub. She'd let me into her life by telling me what was bothering her. Maybe she felt close to me. She could have said thanks and bought me a drink. Not come on to me the way she did. She'd had quite a bit to drink, so maybe that was the answer. She'd lost her inhibitions and thought it would be okay. She knew we never stepped over the line and yet that's what she'd done. I was very confused. It kept going round in my head and I could find no answer for her behaviour.

I decided to sleep on it so I finished my lager and went up to bed. After a week of very early shifts getting up at five, I really needed to sleep.

Ha. A good night's sleep. I managed to get about four hours kip. Most of the night was spent, tossing and turning. I awoke tired and wasn't sure about going to Mel's for our little chat. Still, I went through the motions of getting up and having a long shower. After which I felt a lot better. I went to the café on the way to Mel's for a wake-up cup of coffee. It did the trick and the thirty-minute walk made me feel almost human.

Mel let me in and I headed straight for the kitchen, where we always went. It was two rooms knocked into one and was huge. The focal point of the room was a very large heavy pine table in the middle. It was what Mel called a talking table. She'd bought it a few years ago and had us all carve our names in it, before she had it sealed and polished.

Okay, a talking table is quite simply what it sounds like. No, it doesn't talk, it's where we all sit about and talk. When we go over for our monthly Sunday roasts we never get to the lounge. We end up spending the whole time after dinner sitting round the table talking. In fact I can't remember the last time we actually sat in the lounge. The kitchen is so comfortable and, in the winter, the cosiest place in the house.

When I got into the kitchen there was a bottle of wine open and two glasses ready. I sat and poured us two good glasses full.

"Nice one Mel. I could do with this." I sat down and took a sip. "Wow, this is good."

"Yeah, it's South African, I thought I'd try it for a change." Mel tasted hers. "Mmm oh yes, very nice. Okay, let's get down to it then."

Straight to the point is our Mel. So I related what happened on the dance floor. Leaving nothing out and trying not to add anything either, just told it as it was.

Mel was quiet for a few moments while she got it all clear in her head.

"How do you feel about what happened?"

"Confused, angry, and happy."

"Okay, I can understand the confused and angry, but why happy?"

"If you'd been on the receiving end of the look she gave me, you'd be happy too."

"Why do you think she looked at you like that?" Mel asked getting to the crux of it.

"If she were gay, I'd say it was because she really fancied me and wanted to fuck my brains out."

"But she's not gay, is she? She's straight, married and about to start a family."

"I know and that's why I'm so fucking confused and angry."

"Okay, keep calm, Jess. I understand what's going on for you. How do you feel about Katie since last night?" Mel asked, trying to keep me from exploding. "Has what happened changed the way you see her now?"

"Of course it has. I'll have to make sure I don't dance with her anymore."

"Come on, don't be flip. It doesn't suit you."

"Sorry, all I know is it will be hard going out with everyone now. I'll have to watch how I interact with Katie. I don't want her to feel bad about what happened and I don't want her to stop coming out with us because of it. I suppose what I'm saying is I'll have to ignore it for the sake of everyone and hope that she can too."

It was good talking to Mel. She had a way of getting you to talk your way through the problem and coming to your own conclusions. I guess that's the sign of a good counsellor.

"That's true and I'm sure when Josie chatted with Katie last night, she would have been saying the same things," Mel said. "Moving on from there, I think you've now proved you're completely over Sue."

"You know you're right. If I was prepared to let Katie in then Sue is well and truly in the past," I said, feeling pleased that chapter of my life could now be closed and a new one started. "Right, gay women of Croydon beware. Jess is available again."

"Yeah, well don't go too mad. Take it easy to start with," Mel said.

She was trying to keep my feet on the ground, but I knew I had to make up for lost time.

Chapter Three

SO HERE I am back in the present and lusting after Katie had made me realise I had the freedom to go out on the scene again. But I just couldn't trust anyone so, unfortunately, I had to agree with my little sis on that score. And that's how I'd become a serial monogamist. But Josie wasn't right about me not being over Sue. What was stopping me was Katie and that look she gave me all those months ago. I couldn't get it out of my mind. Not one of the women I'd gone out with had looked at me that way. Yes, I know I'm guilty of lusting after a straight woman, but, hey, I'm not doing anything about it. I think I've been quite restrained under the circumstances. What circumstances? The ones where she comes out with us all the time. Actually, I've not seen Katie for a few weeks now at our get-togethers.

"Where's Katie, I haven't seen her for a while?" I asked Josie at the pub on Wednesday.

"Bill's been offered a promotion that involves them moving to New York," Josie replied.

"Oh right, when do they go then?" I tried hard not to show how much that piece of news affected me.

I'd managed to keep things on an even keel with regard to Katie and the incident on the dance floor. I know it's been nearly five months, but you don't know my sister. She just loves to remind me about it and my many other transgressions.

"Well, they're going on Saturday for a month. They need to sort out housing and everything else involved in a move like that. They should be off a couple of weeks before Christmas."

Shit, that's only three months away. Why did that really bother me? I mean to say, it's not as if Katie and I were actually going to get it together, was it? It was just my wishful thinking. Still, in the long run maybe it would be for the best. At least with Katie that far away I wouldn't lust after her and could move on. But that begs the question—to what?

I needed to chat with Mel. She'd help me get things into perspective. She could be relied upon for keeping 'mum' about everything she heard from us lot. Confidentiality was her middle name.

"Right, we'll have to make sure we give her a good send-off then," I said. I hoped my attempt at trying to sound cool was convincing.

"Yeah, that would be nice. I'm sure she'd love it."

"We'd all love it and it's a good excuse for going on the piss if ever I heard one."

I knew I'd need to get pissed to get through Katie's leaving party.

"Talking of booze, I'll get the next round in. Mel, can you give me a hand please?"

Mel and I went up to the bar.

"Mel, I really need to come round and have a chat. When would be good for you?"

"Well, I'm free tomorrow evening at seven if your shifts allow."

"Yeah, that'd be fine. I'll bring a bottle and a take-away. Will Chinese be okay?" It was a thing with Mel. She wouldn't take payment for giving us lot a counselling session, so we always provided a bottle and a take-away.

"Yeah, Chinese is fine. I wondered how long it would take you to talk about Katie." Mel said, leaning into me so no one else could hear.

You know, I'm sure Josie and Mel must have gone to mind-reading college together. How the hell did she know?

"It was easy really," she said, noting my raised eyebrows. "Since that night at Nexus you've been acting differently. You seem to avoid Katie, so I put two and two together."

She reads minds as well.

"Okay, so I'm an open book. You can read a few more pages tomorrow when I come over."

I know sarcasm is the lowest form of wit, but I was feeling quite stressed about this whole Katie thing. It was becoming a mountain when really it should have stayed a molehill.

"You're not an open book, I'm trained to spot these things, that's all."

"I'm sorry, Mel it's just getting to me a bit."

"Okay, no worries, we'll talk tomorrow."

"The sooner the better."

We took the drinks back to the table.

Josie gave me a strange look when Mel and I got back. It made me wonder if she had tuned in to Mel and what we'd talked about at the bar. I hoped not and I hoped after talking with Mel I'd be able to get this mess sorted. That way Josie need know nothing. Ha! Who was I kidding? She probably knew everything anyway.

The rest of the evening was pleasant enough until I was reminded it was my turn to arrange a weekend away. I love the going away, but don't like the organising. I'd have to put my thinking cap on. Usually twice a year, or more if we could, we'd get together for a weekend away. So far we'd tackled ballooning, pony trekking, rock climbing, cycling, Latin American dancing and photography. Not everyone came, but most of us managed to.

"Okay, I'll organise something. Maybe we can use it as a leaving do to end all leaving do's for Katie."

"Yeah, that sounds good," Shelley agreed.

"All right, but we'll have to make sure that she doesn't know what's going on and thinks it's just another of our weekends away," Lou said.

"True. But she's bound to be suspicious if it's close to her going," Lori said.

"When does she go away for the house hunting trip?" Lisa asked.

"Next Saturday," Josie answered. "If we get all the arrangements done while she's away, we can present her with it when she comes back."

"What, you mean actually tell her it's her leaving do?" Shelley asked.

"No, we can't do that. It'd spoil the surprise," Lou said.

"No, Josie's right. If we don't tell her what it's for, she may cry off. She's missed a few of our pubbing and clubbing nights lately."

I knew what Josie was saying and it seemed to be the ideal solution.

"Okay, I can see the logic," Lou agreed. "But Jess doesn't get out of choosing what we do and where we go, etc."

"It's all right. I'll do it." A light bulb went on in my head. "I may have a great idea that I'm sure everyone will like. I just need to check it out on the net first."

"No lap dancing clubs, please," Shelley said.

Everyone laughed.

Lou had organised a night out in a London club. She booked it in all good faith, but when we got there it was a lap dancing night, not the line dancing night we'd been expecting. All of us gay girlies loved it.

"No, it's nothing like that at all. A colleague at work went on one of these weekends with his wife and they loved it."

I'd whetted their appetites now.

"Let's meet here next Saturday. I'll have all the details by then. Katie will be away, so we can talk about it all night." I got up to go. "Now the worker has to love you and leave you."

As I got outside the pub, I sighed heavily. I didn't know how I managed to get through the evening. It was hard being the one to choose a weekend away as Katie's leaving do. I didn't want her to go, yet I didn't want her to stay. If she stayed I could see it causing problems. One of us had to go. This town wasn't big enough for the both of us.

Wanting something to do before it was time to go to bed, I logged on and searched for "Murder Weekends." There were quite a few, to say the least, but the one I was looking for was "Joy Swift's Original Murder Weekends." Apparently she was the creator of these and they'd been going very successfully for a number of years. She'd also been awarded the MBE for her services to tourism, so they had to be good. I needed one near the end of November and about a fortnight before Katie was to leave for New York.

In a way, I still couldn't believe Katie was going, but it had to happen. The gay fairy was not going to perform the miracle I wanted. Yes, I should have known better than to fancy a straight woman. How many times had I seen it happen? How many letters were there in the gay press about lesbians falling for straight work colleagues? I wondered what it was that drove lesbians to this? Maybe it was that the chase was far more interesting than the catch. Maybe for some it was trying to convert a straight woman, as if being a lesbian is a choice. Who would choose to be considered a pariah in society, abnormal, a figure of ridicule or someone to be spat on or beaten up? I could go on for hours, but I won't. With Katie I think I saw someone with whom I could connect and be great friends. Trouble is, with me, I'd not stop at that. I'd want more, which usually meant jumping into bed. Ah well, no point lusting after her now as she would be gone within three months and I'd probably never get to see her again. At least I would be able to get the process of getting over her started and, hopefully, finished.

Getting back to what I was doing, I finally found what I wanted, the last weekend in November, which would be the ideal time. I sent an email and booked it. I just hoped everyone would be able to make it. I printed off several copies of the details to give everyone on Sunday.

While I was at work the next day, I got a text from Josie to ask if I wanted to go with her to the airport on Saturday morning. She'd arranged with Katie and Bill to take them. I told her I had plans and wouldn't be able to make it. I asked Josie to wish Katie and Bill good luck on their visit. At least it proved my little sis had no idea how I was feeling. I could do without a lecture from her at the moment.

I was glad to be seeing Mel tonight. Maybe she could help me sort this out. I was getting in deep and needed to get out before I drowned. Yes, I know, I was being a tad melodramatic. But, hey, I love being a drama queen every now and again. Doesn't everyone?

Finally, I finished work and got home with enough time for a shower before going to see Mel. We were having an Indian summer, so I dressed in light slacks and a T-shirt. I took my denim jacket for later. I love September. It's usually chilly in the mornings and evenings, but can be quite warm during the day.

I picked up a nice bottle of wine and the Chinese and arrived at Mel's dead on seven.

"Hi, Jess, go through," Mel said. She closed the door behind me.

"Shall we have this wine, or do you have one in the fridge that's nicely chilled?" I asked over my shoulder. I put the Chinese on the table where Mel had laid out two places.

With a flourish Mel produced a bottle of wine from the fridge and replaced it with mine. "Here's one I prepared earlier."

"I knew you'd have one chilled," I said grinning.

"Oh you know me so well."

I unpacked the Chinese and we sat loading up our plates. I was really hungry as I'd only had a sandwich for lunch.

"Okay, Jess, let's have it," Mel said between mouthfuls.

"I'm not sure where to begin. I'm in deeper than I thought with Katie and every time I see her I want her more. She's only got to look at me and smile that smile of hers and I'm lost. When I'm near her it's all I can do not to make my feelings obvious. I smell her perfume and I want to take her in my arms and kiss her. I don't know how I'm gonna cope when she goes," I said, with a lump in my throat. The tears were not far away.

"I don't have an easy answer for you. All I can tell you is you got over Sue and you'll get over Katie." Mel held up her hand to stop me interrupting. "I know it's not going to be easy."

God was she good at this mind reading.

"Don't look surprised. It's obvious what you were about to say."

I had to give her that one. It was exactly what I was going to say.

"Okay, so how do I get over her? I mean it's not as if we've had any kind of relationship."

"In your mind you have. In your mind you've been having a relationship since you first met her."

From the first moment I saw Katie I knew how I felt about her. Even though I knew she was straight and married, I still let myself get in too deep. But it was more than that. I felt a connection with her and I was sure she felt it too.

"I can see now how other lesbians get entangled with straight women," I said bitterly.

"Don't start blaming Katie. She didn't ask to be the object of your affections," Mel said, perceptive as ever.

"Yeah, I know. I have to stop behaving like a love-sick teenager, don't I?"

"That's about the size of it. Just be yourself and try to avoid being around Katie too much without making it obvious that's what you're doing."

"I guess with her going to New York for a month, it won't be too hard. There'll only be a couple of months then she'll be off..." I trailed off trying to keep the tears at bay.

"Just let it out, Jess," Mel said. She got up and put her arm round my shoulders. I turned into her waist and cried.

"I'm sorry, this is really silly. How can I be this bad when I haven't even so much as kissed her?" I said, recovering after my little cry.

Mel handed me a tissue and sat back down. She was quiet and sipped her wine.

"I think that's a question only you can answer," she replied, enigmatically.

"Yeah, I suppose you're right," I said, although I wasn't quite sure what she meant.

I left Mel's and walked home. It was a beautiful clear night and I needed the fresh air. My session with Mel had been good, but I still didn't have any real answers. I suppose I need to run it through my pea-sized brain and see what comes out. What I did know was I would have to be careful and not let my feelings show. I didn't want my little sis giving me the third degree.

Oh, well, only a few months to get through.

"HI, GIRLIES, DO I have a treat for you and for Katie's leaving do," I said. I was clutching the information I'd printed out to my chest to add to the anticipation. I looked at everyone as I handed out the sheets and went to the bar to get a drink.

When I got back there was silence.

"Okay, tell me you hate the idea."

"No, it is brilliant. Count me in," Mel said.

"It's got to be one of the best so far," Josie said. "You've really excelled yourself this time."

"Ooh is that a gold star from teacher?" I said.

"Josie's right, it's one of the best ideas. You said on Wednesday that a colleague and his wife had gone on one, and they enjoyed it so that bodes well for us." Lou said.

"Yeah, Peter couldn't stop talking about it. He said it was hard to work out, but worth it because you knew you'd got your money's worth."

I was really pleased they liked the idea.

"So, can you all make it then?" Now it was crunch time as these weekends weren't cheap.

"You can count me in," Shelley said.

"I'm gonna have to opt out of this one unfortunately," Lori said. "It's my cousin's wedding and I'm maid of honour."

"Oh, Lori, that's a shame. We can't change it either because it's the only weekend that works with Katie going away."

I was disappointed that one of us wasn't going to be able to make it.

"I know, but there's nothing I can do about it. Sorry, ladies."

You could tell she was really gutted not to be going.

"Well, how about the rest of you?" I asked.

"Yeah, I'm definitely up for it," Lisa said. "How much do you want for a deposit?"

"Nothing, I just gave my credit card details to hold the rooms 'til I confirmed how many of us there'd be." I got out a pen and started to write the names on my sheet. "Okay, is there anyone apart from Lori who can't go?"

No one said anything so I wrote the names down and added Katie on the end.

"I'll bunk in with Katie," Josie said.

"Can I share with Shelley?" Lou asked.

"Look, you guys write on my sheet who you want to share with. Don't worry about me, I'll be fine, leave me on my own," I said wiping mock tears from my eyes.

"Worry about you? We don't want to cramp your style," Lisa said.

This was a sad indictment on my life. In their eyes all I seemed to do was have loads of women. Well, that was going to have to change.

"You won't be cramping my style. I've decided to turn over a new leaf." I looked at Josie who gave a little smile of encouragement.

"From now on I'm gonna take things slow and not jump into bed so quickly."

"Oh right, we'll believe it when we see it," Lou joked.

Never a truer statement was said. I have a lousy track record regarding women. It usually consisted of meeting, shagging then dumping, all in the space of a couple of weeks at most. It had to change. At least I was well and truly over Sue. She hadn't entered my thoughts at all. That was a good sign, the bad sign was Katie. I now had to get her out of my thoughts.

"You will, don't worry. I'll prove to you all I can do it." Nice bit of bravado there Jess, now I just had to put my money where my mouth was.

Chapter Four

THE TIME ARRIVED for the Murder weekend. The last two and a half months had flown by.

Katie and Bill found exactly what they wanted in New York and came home with pictures of their new house. Katie was full of it and seemed excited to be going on this adventure. Her enthusiasm was infectious and we all wanted to go with her. She informed us that the house wasn't that big, but we'd all be welcome to come over and stay. As long as we didn't turn up en masse. I've always fancied going to America. Mind you, it's New England rather than New York that really appealed to me, where the leaves turn beautiful colours in autumn, or the fall as the Americans call it. Still, I don't think New York is that far away. Maybe I could combine a visit to Katie with New England. Oh yes, that's really going to help get her out of my mind.

Katie is going to stay at home to start with, so Bill got his way at last. I really can't see her being happy with that for long. She's not a stay-at-home kind of person.

Katie was really pleased with the idea of a murder weekend for her leaving do.

"Hey, guys, that's a fantastic idea. I've always wanted to go on one of those," she enthused.

She read the bumph on it in the pub on the Wednesday before our weekend away.

"Yeah, I must admit it is one of my better ideas." I couldn't resist taking credit for the suggestion.

"Well done, you." Katie smiled at me and I almost fell off my chair.

I'm sure she did it on purpose. She never smiles at anyone else like that. Seriously she doesn't and I'm not making it up.

"Jess can sometimes excel herself."

Was it my imagination or did Josie catch Katie smiling at me? Her voice indicated an underlying tone of — behave yourself Jess.

"What time shall we meet on Friday?" Lou asked.

She was one of the drivers. We decided to take her car and mine as they can hold the seven of us plus our luggage quite comfortably.

"We have to be down for cocktails at seven thirty, so I would think if we leave at three we should make it okay. It's about a two and a half hour drive from here. That'll give you girlies time to put on your lipstick."

Josie laughed. "I'll need more time."

"True." Shelley said.

"What, I'll need more time, you cheeky cow!"

"No, me, I'll need more time." Shelley threw a beer mat at Josie.

"Okay ding, ding end of round one. What time does everyone want to leave then?" I put the ball firmly in their court.

"No, Jess, it's okay. Leaving at three will be fine. I can only get a half day off work," Lisa said.

"Right," I said. "Let's meet at The Bird for three o'clock. Any late comers will have to walk."

So, at last it was all arranged. All we had to do now was decide on our costumes. Each Murder Weekend plot had a theme colour for Friday night and a fancy dress on Saturday. This coming weekend's plot was the colours of the rainbow. How appropriate for us gay girlies. The fancy dress theme was angels. God knows how we were going do that. But then He would know, wouldn't He?

Then it hit me. I'd go as a Hell's Angel. That way I wouldn't have a sheet draped round my shoulders. I needed to look a bit cool. You never know who might be at the hotel. No, Jess, you're not going to pull this weekend. It's Katie's leaving do. It wouldn't be right and there's Josie's challenge as well, but it would be fun!

THE NEXT DAY I searched out my old jeans jacket. I was off until Monday so had time to get things ready for the murder weekend. I rang Lisa to go round the charity shops with me during her lunch break. I needed a brightly coloured top and had nothing in my wardrobe that would suit. Lisa was in the same boat so it was going to be good fun trawling through the charity shops.

"Hey, Jess, what do you reckon on this then?" Lisa called out.

I turned and saw her holding up the most garish top I'd ever seen. It was ideal.

"Way to go, Lisa, that's great. Is there another one there?"

"Yeah, but it's not so bright." She held it up for me.

"That'll do."

She brought it over and we paid for them. It was nice picking up what we wanted and being able to benefit the charity as well. It made me feel good, just like an angel. Yes, I know, pass the bucket.

"I need some chains to go on my jacket and some wings. There's a fancy dress shop in the precinct, let's give them a look."

I started to walk in the general direction.

"Sounds good to me. I'll buy some wings too, I'm feeling too lazy to make them," Lisa said.

"I know what you mean. I'm off for the next couple of days, but just can't be bothered to do it."

I'd normally have a go at making the wings, but really didn't want to. The fancy dress shop had just what we wanted and they only cost a couple of quid, so that was good.

"Have you got time for lunch?" I asked.

"Yeah, I'm on flexitime, so I told the boss I was gonna take an hour and a half today."

"Great, let's pop to the pub then."

After lunch Lisa went back to work and I went to a DIY store and bought some lengths of chain to hang on the jacket and jeans I was going to wear. I knew I had some leather bracelets at home that would go nicely with the costume. Leather bracelets, I hear you exclaim. When they were all the rage I bought some, for no other reason than being a bit of a slave to fashion every now and again. So stop getting ideas.

When I got home I tried it all on, adding a pair of dark sunglasses and leather gloves. Though I say it myself, I looked pretty cool, in a hot sort of way.

THE DRIVE TO the hotel was very pleasant with no problems. I got a route from the Internet, which was really easy to follow. So at least we didn't get lost.

At reception we got our keys for the rooms. The rest of the gang paired off leaving me to go to my room alone, ah sad. No not really. I was looking forward to the solitude. When I got there it was a fairly large one with two queen beds so I laid my stuff for the evening out on the spare bed and put the rest away. I noticed an envelope on the table next to the tea tray and opened it. In it was the itinerary for the weekend. There was also a badge with my name on it. At least we wouldn't have to remember names over the weekend. I mean other people's names. I know mine. Well, most of the time.

I made myself a cup of coffee and checked the time. We had a little over an hour to get ourselves ready for the evening. While I drank my coffee I checked the blurb we'd received. It stated it was Max Hart's retirement do. Max Hart was an actor. There was also a warning: Don't mention the words 'Murder Weekend' or 'murder'. We'll only look at you as though you are completely daft and deny all knowledge of any such thing. I loved the thought that we were all to 'play' for real. It would make for much more fun, that's for sure.

I had a shower and put on my clothes for the reception party.

The top I'd bought in the charity shop clashed beautifully with the bright yellow trousers I'd found lurking in the back of my wardrobe. Just don't ask.

I walked into the bar area to meet up with our gang and the rest of the people here for Max Hart's bash. What a sight greeted me. The sea of bright colours was enough to give anyone a migraine. I thought our group looked particularly good, or was that garish?

Katie had on the tightest dress I'd ever seen. It was a bright red strapless sheath coming to the top of her knees. She had a yellow bag and purple shoes. None of it really matched, but it was the colours of the rainbow. The dress accentuated her figure and made me gasp when I saw her. Josie caught the sound and I quickly covered it with a cough. I knew I would have to keep my cool and so I just complimented everyone on their choice of clothes.

We mingled and chatted and finally went into the dining room to find our seats for dinner. Our entire crowd was on one table with a couple of other people. From what Peter had told me, at least one of the unknowns would be from Max's group.

The meal was excellent and I could quite easily have done an Oliver Twist. Everyone was relaxed and getting on with enjoying the evening. I noticed that several of Max's group were up and down during dinner and wondered if it was part of the weekend. They seemed to be in and out of the room and chatting with each other and the guests.

It was a great evening with a murder coming half way through dinner. One of Max's 'guests' came staggering in with blood oozing from a stomach wound. Loads of people crowded round while an ambulance was called for. After the dying person was taken away we played a game. How bizarre! It was quite amazing how everyone got into the spirit of it so quickly. I mean it's not every day you witness this kind of thing. All the guests were affected by the trauma, but managed to play the game and carry on enjoying themselves.

When a detective came in to tell us the person had died, everyone started to question the people who we thought were suspects, trying to find out where they were and what relationship they had with the deceased. I eventually went to my room at about midnight with my head spinning. Not from alcohol, there didn't seem to be much time to drink with everything going on. I set the alarm on my mobile to get me up in good time for breakfast. I didn't want to be missing out on any of the fun.

I slept very well, probably the result of all the cerebral activity, which I wasn't used to. I got down to breakfast and found there were only two other guests there. I joined them at their table and ordered a full English and coffee. I collected a glass of orange juice from the buffet, which had cereal, fruit, yoghurt and rolls. They certainly did us proud. I was half way through my breakfast when a few more guests wandered in, including some of Max's group. We were able to grill them as to what had gone on the previous evening.

My gang didn't surface until I was on my way to the incident room to check out any clues that might be there. The morning was left for us to do what we wanted. As in all good murder stories, we'd been told by the Police not to leave the hotel. But as it was only a game it was all right to go shopping. It was quite bizarre, as I say, but really good clean fun. We just had to be back in the hotel by twelve thirty for lunch.

I spent quite a while in the incident room trying to understand the sparse clues. I made loads of notes before returning to my room. I decided not to go shopping. I don't do shopping, except for the necessities.

I sat on the bed looking at my notes, none of which made much sense yet. I knew from what Peter had told me there would be at least two or three more murders. He also said there would be several more boards in the incident room filled with stuff that may or may not be useful. I wasn't unduly worried that I was totally confused so far. I felt this was going to have to be a team effort, so I'd get together with the gang later and swap notes.

I made a cup of coffee and settled back on the bed to watch the telly. I knew Josie and the gang would be out hitting the shops. Good luck to them. As I've said before I don't do shopping, I try and avoid it like the plague. I'd been in my room about an hour just chilling when there was a knock on the door. I knew it couldn't be housekeeping as my room had already been done.

I opened the door to find Katie standing there!

"Hi, thought you'd like a bit of company," she said. I reluctantly let her in.

My stomach did a somersault as Katie walked past me. Her perfume was intoxicating. I would have to be really careful especially as we were alone in my bedroom.

"I thought you'd gone shopping with the others," I said.

"No, I didn't fancy it so I thought I'd come and chat with you." She made herself comfy on one of the beds.

This could be dangerous. I tried to gather my thoughts to stop them going where I would have no control, which was easier said than done. My stomach was tumbling over and I felt I was losing the internal battle I was having with myself.

"I was just about to make another coffee. Do you want one?" Did my voice go up several octaves then? Is this how pubescent schoolboys behave in the presence of a beautiful woman?

"Yeah, milk, no sugar, please." Katie said and looked at me. I held her eyes and was lost. I couldn't look away. It was if an invisible force held me captive. Katie smiled seductively. I broke contact. I needed to get some conversation going as I made the coffee.

"So have you got any thoughts on who dunnit?" I asked. I was glad my voice didn't sound as shaky as I felt inside.

"No, nothing at all. What about you?"

"I'm stumped. I guess it's too soon to tell. I expect there'll be another couple of murders before the weekend is over. Peter said there were three on his weekend."

I finished making the coffees and handed one to Katie. It was quite unnerving having her sitting in my room. She looked gorgeous in a tight low-cut vest top and jeans. As soon as I could I would have to get rid of her. I knew if Josie came looking for me it would look bad, and, with my track record, no explanation would pacify my little sis.

She took the mug of coffee from me. "Ta. So, are you enjoying it so far?"

"Yeah, it's really great, how about you? Is this a good leaving do or what?"

"The best. I'd never have thought of doing this. I expected a curry and then on to a club, but this is so much better."

Katie was obviously pleased with the weekend.

"I'm gonna miss you."

"Yeah, we're gonna miss you too," I said.

Katie got up. "No, I'm really going to miss you."

She threw me that look again and moved closer to me. I know, I should have moved away, but I just couldn't get my brain to pass the message to my legs.

"Don't look so worried, I'm only going to give you a hug," she said grinning.

I didn't realise my fear had drawn its technicolour picture on my face.

"No. It's fine. I'm fine. No worries. Hug away." God, why the hell had my cool deserted me? I was definitely acting like a horny teenager on a first date.

She was very close now and I could hear my heart beating faster, or was it Katie's? I knew I should stop this, but I really wanted to hold her and it was only a hug, wasn't it? Katie put her arms round me and pulled me into a hug. I reciprocated and we just held each other. We fitted perfectly together as we had on the dance floor, just like pieces of a jigsaw. God, she smelled good. Her hair was so soft against my cheek as she laid her head on my shoulder. I could smell coconut and immediately fantasised about us on a sun-kissed beach, rubbing oil onto each other's bodies, drinking cocktails and — now wouldn't that be good? She'd obviously just showered using a coconut body wash which is similar to the one I use. She smelt wonderful and I knew I was losing the battle here.

I felt Katie's hands move slowly up and down as she gently caressed my back. I shivered as she touched a very sensitive area and I instinctively pulled her closer. Her leg insinuated itself in between mine and I felt myself getting very hard and wet as I pressed against her thigh. Every nerve was ultra-sensitive and it wouldn't take much to push me over the edge. Katie pushed herself in to me and my stomach clenched. Oh, God, I was losing it big time now. She relaxed her hold and pulled away enough to kiss my neck then up to my cheek. I was paralysed. No, I'm lying. I was enjoying it and wasn't going to move to stop her. She touched her lips gently against mine, so soft like a butterfly's wings, and then looked at me for my reaction. I was sure the look on my face said I wanted more, and I know my lips were begging for more. I didn't have to wait, Katie kissed me again, her tongue gently pushing its way in between my lips. I needed no more encouragement and kissed her back. Oh, what a kiss! Our tongues explored the softness of each other's mouths. I groaned and Katie pushed herself further against my thigh and began to move against me. We held each other tightly as our kissing became more urgent. I wasn't sure I could remain standing for much longer. I moved against Katie's thigh. We were both breathing erratically and our kisses became more demanding.

Katie could really kiss. Her tongue was doing the tango with mine and I loved it. I don't know how long we were kissing, time didn't matter. I felt Katie undoing the buttons on my shirt, which she managed without breaking her lips away from mine. I was becoming more aroused and wanted to feel Katie's soft skin against mine, to feel her inside me. Nothing else mattered. All I wanted to do was kiss Katie all over. Touch her. Taste her. Make love to her. I brought my hands to the bottom of her low-cut vest top and began to pull it up. I was aching with need for her it was all too much. I broke the kiss and looked her in the eyes.

"Jesus, Katie, what are you doing to me?" I touched my forehead to hers and held her hands by her sides.

All of a sudden I heard Josie's voice.

"I knew you'd never get past first base with the challenge," she said.

How the hell did she get in?

I stopped what I was doing and pulled away from Katie,

looking around the room as I did my buttons up. There was no one here but Katie and me, it was all in my head. It worked though and Josie's voice was right. If I hadn't heard it I would've jumped into bed with Katie and to hell with the consequences.

"What's wrong, Jess? Why did you stop? Didn't you like kissing me?"

She had to be kidding. Of course I liked kissing her.

"Yes. No. I mean — look it shouldn't have happened."

I was glad it had, but now it made things that much harder for me. I was falling for Katie before the weekend and now kissing her had made it worse. How could I have been such a fool?

"It did happen and I've got to say I'm not sorry. I really enjoyed kissing you."

"Yeah okay, but why did you kiss me? You're married, about to go to New York and start a family. You're straight and I'm gay."

I was beginning to get angry now. I was coming to my senses and the reality of this hit me. I had nearly committed adultery.

"It was just a kiss," Katie said, trying to calm me down.

I was pacing the room now. It may have been just a kiss to her, but to me it was more than that. It was going to be hard to get over this. I was confused, angry and upset that I'd let it get this far. Mind you, I couldn't have stopped it happening. It was as inevitable as night following day.

"No, it wasn't just a kiss. We were gonna make love, weren't we? What did you think you were doing? Trying it out with a woman before you go? Did you read a magazine in the hairdressers? Did it say how straight women are getting it on with their friends? Did it say how it was all right to experiment?"

Boy was I getting on one now and I couldn't stop the tirade or the pacing.

"So you carry out your experiment. Then go swanning off to New York to your straight life, having sampled lesbian sex. Yeah, you enjoyed it, but wouldn't want to repeat it. Is that what you'd tell your new friends at brunch eh, that you did it with a woman? Meanwhile, I'm left here wondering what the hell happened. I would be just another lesbian used for the furtherance of the great straight woman's education. So she can be part of the in-crowd. So you go off to New York, leave me trying to put all those worms back into the can you've just opened!"

I must admit I did go overboard, just a tad. I guess I was angrier with me than Katie. I knew the signs, but I had let my libido take over. I should have kept my distance. Yes, I love to play it safe, not. I folded my arms, trying to protect myself a bit late for that now.

I looked at Katie. She was stunned by my outburst. I saw the hurt in her eyes and felt guilty. What a fucking mess.

"Look, I think you'd better go," I said. "Let's just forget it happened."

Forget it happened? As if I could do that any time soon. I was calmer now, but still angry that I'd let things get so far.

Katie was quiet and we just looked at each other. She searched my eyes, but I kept them neutral. She moved toward me, but I backed away. I had to keep distance between us. Katie stopped and I could see she was confused. Yes, well, she wasn't the only one.

Katie moved toward the door. "Jess, I'm so sorry. Can we still be friends? Please?"

I saw the pleading in her eyes. Apart from what just happened we had become good friends. I could see she didn't want to think she'd jeopardised that. And what would it do to the group dynamics if we were not our usual selves?

"Yeah, sure," I answered with a wan smile.

I opened the door and made sure the coast was clear. The last thing I wanted was to find Josie outside. There was nobody in the corridor so I let Katie out.

"See you for lunch?" she asked as she went out.

"Yeah, see you down there."

I went back into my room and closed the door behind her. I leaned against it, and slid down until I was sitting with my head slumped on my knees and started to cry. I'm not sure why. Maybe it was because I'd wanted to make love with Katie and I couldn't. Maybe I was angry that I'd let myself down by my total lack of control after I'd told Josie I would be able to handle the challenge. I was so mixed up after what had happened.

I got up, wiped my eyes and sat in the chair. What did it all mean? Was Katie gay after all? Or was it just as I'd ranted at her that she was trying it out, to see what it was like? The questions kept going round in my head with no real answers that I could think of. Everything pointed to her being gay. If she'd been trying it out I think she would have done it that night when we were at the club and she was a little drunk. She could then at least blame it on the booze. But this was broad daylight and we were both sober, so no excuse except for the one where she's emigrating and so she feels she can get away with anything. But it's still adultery isn't it, even though it's with another woman and not a man? I know I'm not a fan of Bill, but I wouldn't do that to him. But was kissing still adultery? If it was I was in deep doggy doo-doo.

The more I thought about kissing Katie the more I realised that kissing is a very intimate act, more so perhaps than actually having sex. I enjoyed kissing Katie and I wanted to do it again and never stop. I wanted to feel her soft lips against mine and I wanted to explore the inside of her mouth and feel her react to my kisses. I didn't want to have sex with Katie, I wanted to make love with her. I was getting in too deep and felt the longing in me awakening after being dormant for so long. That was the really scary thing, knowing that my feelings for Katie ran deeper than pure lust. I had never felt this way before, even with Sue, which was a little bit sad in retrospect.

I looked at my watch and saw it was nearly midday. The hotel bar would be open by now and I could really do with a drink. I quickly washed my face, tidied myself up and went to the bar.

Chapter Five

I ORDERED A whisky and a pint then parked myself at a table. I knocked the whisky straight back and it really hit the mark. I drank the lager more slowly as I didn't want to be out of it at this time of the day. I was sitting reading my notes when Mel joined me.

"Hi, solved it yet?" she asked as she sat down.

"No chance. It's not gonna be that easy. Peter said they had three whatsits, loads of clues and he still didn't get it." I remembered not to say the m word.

Mel gave me one of her appraising looks.

"You don't look so good. What's wrong?"

"I'm fine, just a bit tired," I lied.

"Don't give me that, Jess. I know there's something wrong. I can see it in your face. Spill the beans."

Mel knew there was something wrong and was not going to give up. It would be easier in the long run to just tell her.

"Katie came to my room this morning. We kissed and I nearly ended up in bed with her."

"Jesus, Jess, how did that happen?"

Personally I would have thought it was obvious, but I didn't say that to Mel. I knew what she really meant.

"It just did and now I'm so confused, and before you ask, Katie came on to me. I must admit I didn't turn her down, until I heard Josie's voice in my head that is." I laughed at the absurdity of it.

"What do you mean Josie's voice?"

I think Mel was worried for my sanity, hearing voices in my head.

"What did she say?" Mel was starting to grin as well.

I explained to her about Josie's challenge and how I was determined to go through with it.

"It's about time you settled down. Serial monogamy isn't your style," Mel said. "At least Josie's challenge is working if it stopped you in your tracks."

"True." I took a sip of my beer. "Josie's right, I do need to take things slower. I should get to know someone before I jump into bed with them."

"Okay, so how do you feel about Katie trying to seduce you?" Mel asked. "Wait, let me get a drink first. It'll give you time to think. Coffee for you though, can't have you getting pissed before lunch." She looked at the empty whisky glass.

She went to the bar to order our drinks.

I did as she suggested and gave some thought to this morning. I really enjoyed kissing Katie, but that wasn't the point at all, was it? So maybe it wouldn't be that much of a problem. Yes, right! Mind you, if I hadn't heard Josie's voice I know we would have ended up making love. I really wanted her, I knew that much. The more I thought about it the more I realised I was falling for her. It had nothing to do with sex. Okay, yes it did. But it was more to do with deeper feelings. I longed for her. I needed her and I wanted to be the only one in her life. None of this could happen because she was straight, wasn't she? Perhaps it was just as well she was leaving. God only knows what would happen if she stayed. Yes, well, I knew what would happen. Sooner or later one of us would get hurt, and that one would probably be me.

Mel returned with the drinks.

"Well, have you thought about it?" She sat down.

"Yeah, I have and I know I'm falling for Katie big time. If I hadn't heard Josie's voice I would have gone to bed with her and it isn't really just about sex. There's more to it."

Mel, being the good counsellor that she is, waited for me to continue, as she knew I would.

I took a sip of my coffee. "I guess it's for the best she's leaving. If she stayed things would be even harder. As it is I don't know how I'm gonna get over her. How can I have been so stupid as to let this happen?"

"Let's not get into that," Mel said. "When we get back you're going to have to avoid seeing Katie. I know it'll be hard, but it's only for a couple of weeks."

"Won't it look a bit strange if I don't go out with everybody? Especially as it's only two weeks before she leaves. We'll all be making the most of the time before she goes. It will certainly make Josie's antennae hone in on me if I'm not around."

"Mmm, I suppose you're right. Okay then, just make sure you're never alone with her. Keep everything on a friendly level, but don't overdo it."

"So go back to how it was before. Just being good friends."

I could see what Mel was saying and knew she was right. It was important I kept everything as normal as possible. Josie was already a little suspicious after the dance floor incident. I had to make sure I didn't fuel those suspicions.

"That's exactly what you have to do. It won't be easy but it's not for long. I take it you won't be coming to the airport to see Katie and Bill off?"

"No. I managed to change shifts so I can legitimately say I'm working."

"Nice one."

Mel reached over to grab my notebook.

"The others have just walked in," she whispered, as she opened the book. "So, how far have you got?"

I picked up on her cue. "Nowhere really. You got any ideas then?"

"Hi, you two, have you solved it then?" Lisa sat down at the table.

"Nope we were just saying we hadn't got a clue yet," Mel said.

"Well, maybe there'll be more whatsits and clues to make it clearer," Josie said.

"Yeah right. Oh look! I saw a pig fly right past the window," Lisa chimed in, pointing.

Everyone laughed.

We sat drinking and chatting before we went into the dining room.

Lunch was a buffet affair during which the afternoon game was explained. Whilst we were eating, two of the characters had a stand-up row, and of course we all took notes.

Afterwards we went into the public area of the hotel to play the game. It involved clues that were pinned in various places. We had to guess the name of famous people from these clues. It sounds easy, but it was a game where you really had to think. Each of the clues was divided into two parts. The first clue was for the first name and the second for the surname. Sometimes, if you got the first one you could guess the second. There were forty in all and we split up to meet back in the bar and compare notes.

About half a dozen of the clues were down the walls of the stairs and on into a small open area where the toilets were. After all the liquid I'd consumed I was desperate for a wee.

I went in and left my answer sheet by the sinks. I was just about to close the cubicle door when I decided to grab the answer sheet and I took it in with me. Can't be too careful. You never knew who could walk in and crib the answers.

I completed my toilet break with the sheet in my mouth and still had it there while I washed my hands. I was about to leave when I heard a toilet flush and the door of one of the cubicles opened.

"Hi, Jess."

It was Katie and I got that familiar thump in my stomach as I looked at her. Oh boy.

"Hi," I mumbled with the sheet in my mouth, which I removed quickly. "Sorry, hi, how are you doing with the clues?"

"I've got a few answers and some half answers."

We stood looking at each other. I could feel Katie's eyes

reaching right inside me, searching my soul. My legs felt like jelly. I wasn't sure I would be able to walk away even if I wanted to, and I wasn't sure I did.

Katie broke the spell.

"Look, are you all right after this morning?"

"Oh yeah, of course I am." However, I was uncomfortable talking about it.

"I'm sorry you may be able to forget it happened, but I can't," she said.

She looked really great in the low-cut vest top that I'd nearly removed earlier. I'd love to see her out of it. I mentally shook my head in an effort to bring me back to reality. But, to be honest, I've got the will power of a stunned rat.

Katie moved closer to me. Here we go again *déjà vu* and I still couldn't move my legs, although I must admit I didn't try very hard. Yes, definitely weak. I should go. I should go. The words became a mantra inside my head. Oh, what the heck, what harm could another kiss do? Yes, I know I was only saying to Mel how it was going to be hard getting over Katie. It's okay. I won't make the first move. Though I suppose in a way I did as I was mentally willing Katie to kiss me. That way I could justify it later, but knew I was going to pay for it. I blame it on the alcohol myself. I was feeling reckless now. I never could take afternoon drinking.

She put her hands on my shoulders and pushed me into a vacant cubicle and locked the door behind us. Well, she did make the first move. I took her face in my hands and started to kiss her. She responded by pulling me into a clinch and kissing me back passionately. God, I was lost in that kiss. It was intense and demanding, but it wasn't just that. It felt so right. It was as if I'd come home. So how could it be wrong?

Suddenly I was brought back to my senses by the main door to the toilets opening. Katie had heard it too because she stopped and pulled away from me. Whoever it was had lousy timing. Katie put her fingers to her lips to indicate we should be completely quiet. No argument from me on that one.

We heard the cubicle door next to us open and close, then the lock drawn across. A few minutes later the toilet was flushed and whoever it was came out. We could hear water running into the sink.

Katie flushed our toilet, pushed me to the back corner of the cubicle, opened the door and went out pulling it closed behind her.

"Hi, Josie, how are you doing with the game?" I heard Katie ask.

"Oh, not too bad I suppose. How about you?"

"Yeah, the same but I've got a few answers. Let's go up and

compare notes," Katie said.

Nice one.

I heard the door open and close, but I waited for a few minutes before coming out. The coast was clear. I saw my answer sheet by the sinks where I'd put it when Katie came in. Jesus, what was I doing letting Katie kiss me again? Who was I kidding? I wanted it as much as she obviously did. Anyway, I was definitely going to blame it on the booze, and I was definitely not going to think about adultery. Shows how reckless I was feeling after a couple of drinks. As I said, I'm not good with afternoon drinking. That's my excuse and I'm sticking to it.

I WENT OUT and up to the bar, working out a couple more of the answers on the way. I joined the rest of the gang once I'd got myself a drink. If this carried on I was going to become an alcoholic. Still, it gave me the perfect excuse for kissing Katie, at least in my head it did.

"So how are we doing?" I asked, maybe a little more cheerfully than was safe.

We compared notes and filled in one sheet with all the answers we'd managed to get. We were going to enter as a team, which was easier than filling out seven sheets. There were four questions none of us had been able to work out.

"I'll have another look at number ten if you guys pair off and take the other three," Josie said.

Number ten was quite involved and Josie loved a challenge. It was a pig and she was welcome to it.

"I've got an idea about the first name," she continued as she got up, "so if I study it I might be able to get the surname."

"Okay, but we need to get a move on. We've only got ten minutes left," Lisa said. "Come on Mel, you're clever. You can be with me and we'll tackle number forty two."

"I'll go with Shelley to number twenty eight, which leaves Katie and Jess number thirty five," Lou said.

Everyone got up and rushed off to give the clues one more try.

"Right, Jess, let's get to it. I'm sure between us we can solve it," Katie said as she grabbed me by the hand and pulled me up.

Her touch, oh my God, I couldn't get enough of this woman. I was in danger of losing my sense of right and wrong.

"Take it easy, I'm coming." I laughed.

We stood looking at the clue, but nothing came to mind. Though I must admit that my mind was elsewhere and not totally on the problem at hand. Maybe it was because I was enjoying the view of Katie's cleavage, as she stood close. There was another

couple checking out the clue as well, hence the closeness. Don't
worry, I wasn't staring. Well, not much. It was just the angle she
was standing at. I couldn't help but get a great view and, hey, I
never look a gift horse in the mouth.

There was one half of me enjoying it and the other half
thinking how wrong it was. I suppose being away for a weekend is
a different place mentally as well as geographically. Maybe it was
because of this that we'd allowed ourselves to be reckless and to
enjoy it. I knew we had to be careful in case anyone, especially
Josie, noticed. The trouble would start when we returned to reality,
when we got back home, where I knew I would feel guilty about
what Katie and I were doing. Even though I knew I'd never have
sex with her, wasn't kissing equally as bad? Yet I didn't feel guilty,
even knowing it would hurt Bill. I knew I was being reckless. What
he didn't know couldn't hurt him and that wasn't me at all. I never
ever went with someone who was still attached. It was a big no-no
with me. I knew I was being totally irresponsible, but for now I
didn't care. I would when we got back, but for now I was going to
go with the flow and relax and enjoy it. I knew it wasn't going to
last and if I'd got to get over Katie a few more kisses couldn't make
it any worse could it? In for a penny and all that jazz.

"I can't get this one, can you?" I asked Katie.

"No, it's really got me. Let's go back to the bar," she said.

I looked at my watch. "No, we'd better go straight in for
afternoon tea."

"I'm still full-up after lunch."

"Yeah, I know what you mean, but it's only tea and cakes, I'm
sure we can manage that."

"Okay, let's go."

By the time we got there the rest of the gang were seated and
just getting the tea poured. None of them had any luck either. We
were four answers short, but it seemed we weren't the only ones.

When the answers were given out you could hear "of course"
and "oh yeah," to the ones everyone had trouble with.

Then another murder was discovered, so we spent time
questioning suspects and checking for more clues in the incident
room.

I went to my room with only an hour to spare to get ready. The
others had gone earlier, but I had a theory running around in my
head that I'd wanted to check out.

Once in my room I showered and got ready in record time.
Mind you, I don't bother with make-up and the like so it doesn't
take me long. Don't get me wrong I don't have anything against
make-up, it's just I can't be bothered with it, or faffing around with
my hair. After I'd got my angel costume on I surveyed myself in the

full-length mirror. I looked great, even though I say it myself.

WHAT A SIGHT greeted me when I got to the bar, angels galore. It was great how inventive some people had been. Everyone had made the effort and there were all sorts of angels and yes, even an "Allsorts" angel.

Katie's fallen angel was really something. She had on a bright red crop top that left a wide swathe of silky-smooth flat tanned and toned stomach. She'd teamed this with the shortest black mini-skirt, which was more like a belt. Underneath the mini-skirt were stockings and red suspenders. Her halo was black as were her wings. God, she looked gorgeous. I just hoped nobody could read my thoughts, because they were certainly X-rated. I could imagine running my hand up her stocking clad leg to the expanse of bare thigh at the top and then to—I had to stop thinking like that, it was making me hot and I still had dinner to get through sitting at the same table as Katie.

When we got to our table for dinner the seating plan had me next to Katie. I had no chance to change the names around. But then again, I thought it would probably be safer to sit next to her. If she were opposite I would spend most of the evening staring at her. As it was I would probably be in a constant state of painful arousal.

It was really funny watching all the angels trying to arrange their wings as they sat down. I was glad I'd opted for a costume that had smaller wings rather than the big ones a lot of the guests were sporting.

Dinner was fantastic and afterwards we played a music game. Our table won and the prize was a small cuddly teddy each. Then it was time for dancing and judging the fancy dress.

The DJ played a variety of music that suited everyone. He played a section of Latin American, which was great for us. We'd been on a Latin American dance weekend a few months ago and had learnt the cha-cha, the samba and the tango. We weren't brilliant but we could do a passable impression of the dances.

Everyone got up, I grabbed Katie's hand and we went to the dance floor for the tango. If I was going to go down, then it was going to be big time. Besides, on the Latin American weekend, Katie and I'd paired up and were quite good at it, the dance that is. To answer your question, it was before the night at Nexus, a time when we were just friends.

The tango is a very sexy dance and I knew it would get very hot out there. After stumbling a bit at the start, we really got into it. I was totally lost in the dance to the exclusion of everyone else. Katie had a lot to do with it as well, but I love the tango and Latin

American music. She felt so good in my arms as we danced. I think we must have cleared a space because suddenly we had a lot of room to dance. Our bodies were so close at times we were moving almost as one, I was really enjoying it then the music finished and we did the final twirl.

At that moment everyone applauded. It seems we were the only ones dancing, everyone else was watching. I suddenly came over all embarrassed. Yes I know, hard to believe. I scuttled back to the table and downed half my drink in one go. Dancing like that is such thirsty work. I looked up and saw Josie heading straight for me. I couldn't read her look in the subdued lighting, but I'm sure it wasn't good. Fortunately Mel intercepted her. She grabbed Josie's arm and took her for a dance.

I took my cue and went to the ladies where I stood leaning against the wall for what seemed like ages, mulling things over. I'd let myself get in deeper than I should. Okay, okay, don't even bother to say I told you so. Finally I stopped beating myself up, splashed cold water on my face, and hoped Katie wasn't going to come in while I was there. I had to back off and be strong. The trouble is, as I said before, I have the will power of a stunned rat.

When I got back to the table everyone was up dancing except Mel. I sat down next to her.

"Thanks for heading off Josie," I said. "You don't need to tell me, I know it's a mess."

"I wasn't. I can see what's going on. I suppose you feel you can behave differently because you're away from home and so you've decided to be hung for a sheep as well as a lamb."

"What do you mean?"

"Well, you've had one kiss in your room this morning and I'm betting it wasn't the last," she said. "So you reckon, if you've had one kiss, another and another isn't going to be much worse."

I laughed. "Are you sure you weren't a mind reader in a previous life?"

"Jess, you need to be really careful. Josie's getting suspicious." Mel was serious now.

"I expected you to tell me to stop," I said.

"And what good would that do? You know very well telling someone to stop doing something is a sure way to get them to carry on."

"True. I do know what you're saying and I do get it. The weekend's nearly over and after it is, I promise I'll steer clear of being alone with Katie," I said, trying to convince myself I could actually do it.

"Mmm, you're on a reckless streak at the moment and I think you're enjoying the danger a little too much," she said. "I'm going to get another drink."

Mel could really get into my head and she was right, I was enjoying the danger and the excitement. But most of all I was enjoying being with Katie, even though I knew my arousal would not be assuaged any time soon, at least not by Katie. However, I was determined not to let it go any further than kissing. I was taking this weekend in isolation, like it didn't count and wasn't real. Yes, who was I kidding? Of course it was real, of course I was going to get hurt. I was tough, though, and I could handle it, couldn't I? Or was I heading for a really big fall? Yes, of course I was, but just how hard was I going to land? Pretty hard I guess, deep down I knew that, but I was prepared to take the risk. I got over Sue didn't I? Okay, so it hurt like hell, but I still got over her. What the hell, life's too short. But if that was the case, why wasn't I prepared to go to bed with Katie? That was the million-dollar question I already knew the answer to. It wasn't that silly challenge, it was more. It wasn't the fact that I didn't want to commit adultery because in a way kissing Katie was just that, in my eyes at least. It was more than that. I had a deep longing for Katie. I now knew I felt much more for Katie than I was previously prepared to admit. Or, maybe I knew I was going to have to get over her when she went away. I just thought sleeping with her would complicate things. Yes, I know, they're already complicated. Oh, I can't explain it. Maybe I thought of Katie as more than just a weekend fling. No, I knew it was much more than that. She was worth more than that and so was I.

I was brought out of my self-analysis by loud screams. Then a bloodied body fell into the dining area. God, it's all go on these murder weekends.

It was gone midnight again before I got back to my room. I was knackered from the fun and games and I don't just mean the murders. It was a really great weekend and I made a mental note to organise another.

I stripped off my angel outfit and had a long shower. I could have stayed there for hours with the water massaging my body. I towelled myself dry, put on a bathrobe, and poured myself a can of lager from my private little stash. Do you know how expensive drinks in mini bars are? Could have done with being a bit cooler, but hey, you can't have everything.

I felt quite decadent lounging on the bed in my robe with a drink in my hand. I switched off all the lights and opened the curtains a bit to let a little of the street light in. It was so restful on the eyes and very quiet, until a knock at the door broke into that.

I knew who it would be, but thought I'd check just in case it was Mel or Josie. I peeked through the spy-hole and sure enough it was Katie. There was no way I was letting her in, with me almost naked. Yes, maybe I'm being a spoilsport but it's all right for you guys. I'm the one who's going to come down with a bump when I get home.

I crept quietly back to the bed and sat down again.

There was another knock, slightly louder and longer. I ignored it again. After five minutes or so there was nothing, so I went to have another look. The corridor looked empty so I took a chance that Katie had gone to her room and looked outside. It was all clear. In a way I was disappointed, but it was for the best. Although I'd had fun and enjoyed kissing Katie, I knew I had to try and get back to the real world, not this fantasy I was living. Reality was going to hit big time on the drive back home. I'm going to need a few wine and take-away sessions with Mel. Best make sure I book her for at least the next six months.

Chapter Six

NEXT MORNING AFTER breakfast we all went to the incident room to check on the clues. We had to hand our solutions in by eleven thirty. It was going to be difficult to sort out any kind of solution at all. It was a complicated plot with lots of twists and turns. But then if it'd been too easy it wouldn't have been as much fun. We spent nearly an hour looking at the clues, by which time our heads were spinning. It made me realise being a copper is not at all how it's portrayed on the television.

We decided to pay our bills and get our luggage packed and in the cars. Once that was done we'd have the time to sit and work on what our solutions were going to be.

I was the last one to the car park and found Lou had already packed her car. She and her passengers were going to the incident room first, and then we were to meet in the bar to confer.

I saw Shelley and Katie waiting by my car. Shelley was okay, but not Katie. Then I realised it was logical. Lou and I were going to drop everyone home, not at The Bird. Katie lived about ten minutes from me and would be the last drop on the journey, convenient or what? I hoped she didn't have an ulterior motive, or did I?

I put Katie's cases and mine on the bottom with Shelley's on top for ease of access when I dropped them both off. Was it my imagination or did Katie wink at me conspiratorially as she handed me her case? I wasn't looking forward to the journey home.

We all met in the incident room and discovered we were no nearer to finding out who'd committed the murders. I studied the clues and grilled the cast, but felt I was getting nowhere. I didn't know who dunnit and was beginning not to care. I had other things on my mind.

"Let's go to the bar and talk about it," I said to everyone.

"Okay, sounds good to me. I could do with a coffee to stimulate the brain cells," Lou said.

"It's all we'll get this time of the morning," Lisa said.

"Shame, I need a whisky to stimulate my brain cells." Shelley sounded disappointed.

"You'll have to make do with coffee," Mel teased.

We sat down at two tables we'd pulled together. Our coffees steaming almost as much as our brains.

"Anyone got any clue at all?" Josie asked.

"I think the butler did it," Lisa replied.

"No, I think it was the downstairs maid," Shelley said.

"Come on guys, let's be serious," I said above the hubbub.

"Why? You never are," Mel said.

True.

"Well, this time I am," I said, putting on my serious face. It didn't last. I cracked and everyone laughed.

We did the best we could with our solutions, but when it came to the denouement we were completely off base. If we'd combined all our theories we may have come close. But we reckoned we might stand a better chance by putting all seven in. Ah well, better luck next time.

THE DRIVE HOME was uneventful except for a bit of banter regarding who dunnit and why. We all agreed that it was a great weekend and one that should be repeated.

"It's a shame I'll miss the next one," Katie said.

"Well, if you let us know when you'll be coming for a visit we can arrange one for when you're over," Shelley said.

"Yeah," I agreed. "That would be a great idea and a good excuse for a weekend away."

We arrived at Shelley's and got her bags out.

"See you next week then?" Shelley said, as she picked up her bags.

"Okay," I said.

"Bye, Katie. Will you be out at all before your final drink-up?" Shelley asked.

"Not sure at the moment, but I definitely will be for that night."

"All right, see you guys." Shelley made her way to her front door.

I got back in the car and we drove in silence to Katie's.

I pulled up outside her house and got her bags out of the boot.

"Come in for coffee," Katie said.

"Yes, please. I could do with using your loo. I've drunk so much coffee I don't think I'll even make it the short distance home without peeing myself," I replied.

Katie grinned as she let us both in.

"It's upstairs and first on the left." She dumped her bags in the lounge.

"Ta."

I went up.

Katie had just finished making the coffee when I got to the kitchen and I noticed she'd poured herself a large white wine.

"I didn't fancy anymore coffee. I know you're driving so I

didn't pour you one," she said, as I sat down at the table.

Her house was a large semi. The kitchen had been extended into a kitchen diner to allow a dining table and six chairs for entertaining. I'd never been here before. The couple of times she'd had us lot round, I'd been working.

I began to feel uncomfortable being alone with Katie in her home. It wouldn't have been so bad if it were the pub or my house. But here I was on her turf. I could always leave though couldn't I? I didn't have to stay.

"Well, I thought that was a great weekend," Katie said, breaking into my thoughts.

"Yeah, I really enjoyed it."

A grin spread across Katie's face.

I could read Katie's thoughts as I watched her grinning from ear to ear. I must admit I wanted to do the same as I'd really enjoyed the weekend too and not just the murders. But now it was time for a reality check.

"Look, the weekend is over and what happened is also over. You know, it's a — what happens in Vegas stays in Vegas — kind of thing," I said. I wanted to get things back to where they were before we went away, even though I knew that was probably impossible.

"The weekend's not over yet," Katie said. "Bill won't be back until tomorrow."

Was she suggesting what I thought she was? Did she think I was a complete bastard to do anything in their marital home? My fault for letting it get this far, giving out misleading signals. How did I think Katie would react? God, what a mess. I knew it was going to hit me, I just didn't think it would be this soon.

"Katie, I don't care when Bill gets home. I told you what happened during the weekend is over. I go back to what I said before. You're straight and I'm gay," I said harshly. "I can't believe I let it happen," I said, almost to myself.

"You wanted to kiss me and you wanted more. Why don't you just admit it?" Katie was getting angry now.

She was right, I did want more and I was beginning to realise just how much more and Katie looked so sexy when she was angry. Oh, God, here I go again. I needed to keep my hormones in check. Maybe I need to put something in my coffee.

"Jess, I don't know what's happening to me. I'm confused about my feelings," Katie said. Her eyes full of confusion searched mine for the compassion I felt sure she expected to see.

Was she playing with me, hoping to trick me into bed? I wasn't sure, but I did know I couldn't go down that route. I couldn't have sex with Katie, be her experiment. What about Bill? I may not like him, but I'm not going to do that to him.

"Fine, but don't expect me to fuck you so you can see what it's like. You cannot sort your feelings out at the expense of mine!" I shouted at her. "I'm going now. I think it's best if we don't see each other until your leaving drink-up. I don't trust myself not to get angry and I don't want anyone else to know what's been going on."

"Nothing's been going on, you made sure of that!"

"And why do think that was?" I asked her.

I got up ready to leave and stood looking at her waiting for her answer. None was forthcoming so I walked out and shut the door behind me.

I drove home slowly, trying to calm myself down. How could I have been such a prat? I'd make sure I was busy until Thursday week. I was far too angry to be in her company without letting something slip. That wouldn't be good for either of us because if Josie got a sniff of it, my life wouldn't be worth living.

To be fair, I was angrier with myself than Katie. How could I have let my attraction to her get so far? I suppose I couldn't really blame her. If she was genuinely confused about her feelings, then I was an easy solution. She had an itch and she thought I would scratch it.

OVER THE NEXT week and a half I was busy so didn't have to lie. I'd been caught for a couple of shift changes that worked out nicely. So when Thursday came it was the first time I'd seen everybody since the Murder Weekend. I was calmer too, as I'd seen Mel in a professional capacity to try and get things into perspective, and that had helped a little.

"Hi, everyone, you all got a drink?" I asked, as I joined them at The Bird.

"Yeah, fine ta. Haven't seen you for so long, I'd almost forgotten what you looked like," Lisa joked.

"Ha, ha, very funny. I'll put a photo in the post for you," I said, giving her a dig in the ribs.

"You're just in time for the presentation," Josie said.

We'd all put money in and bought Katie a digital camera. Now she can take loads of pictures and email them to Josie who'd pass them on.

"Well, Katie, the time has come for us to bid you a fond farewell," Lou started.

"We thought the best present would be one that we could all enjoy," Shelley added.

"So, here it is and you'd better use it lots," Lori said.

She handed Katie the nicely wrapped box. Must have been Josie who wrapped it, she's so good at stuff like that. I tend to use half a roll of Sellotape when I try to wrap presents.

When Katie opened it the tears started to flow down her cheeks.

"Oh, don't go soppy on us," Mel said. "You'll start us all off."

"Sorry guys this is such a good idea. I've always wanted one so thanks so much and, yes, I'll use it lots. You'll get fed-up with the amount of pictures I'll be emailing," she said, and promptly burst into more tears.

Everyone crowded round and we had a group hug.

"All right everyone break it up! Let's get this show on the road," Josie shouted.

"Yeah, let's get off to Nexus and have a good time," Lisa said.

Thursday nights at Nexus are usually quiet but that wasn't going to bother us lot. We were going to make the most of the night. I can't remember the last time I'd been there on a Thursday. Still, it was Katie's night and I was pleased that I'd decided to be there. There were a few times in the last couple of weeks when I'd almost cried off and I bet that would have really got Josie's brain cells on overtime working that one out.

We walked to Nexus, all chatting loudly. I was striding out ahead as I usually did when Katie caught me up and linked arms with me.

"Are you all right?" She asked.

I could hear the uncertainty in her voice. She sounded so vulnerable I wanted to hold her and tell her everything was okay. Don't worry, I didn't.

"I am, are you?"

"Yeah, I was just worried that I've ruined our friendship by being stupid," she said quietly.

I laughed out loud. "It's all right I'm not laughing at you. I'm just trying to stop Josie getting the wrong idea. Laugh as well, please?"

She did and I joined her.

"You haven't ruined anything, things just got out of hand. Let's just pretend it never happened and have a good night."

"Okay, I just don't want to lose your friendship," she said.

I wanted to tell her she'd never lose my friendship. She'd never lose my love, and I'd never forget what happened. But I didn't, that was something I would keep to myself.

By this time we'd arrived at Nexus, piled in and sat at one of the large tables. I went to the bar and gave the barman the money we'd all put in for drinks.

"Let me know when that gets low and we'll have a whip round," I told him, and ordered the first round.

It was still early and the place was quite empty, so we had

plenty of room to dance and have a laugh. Within an hour or so it began to fill up a bit.

I was up at the bar again getting the next round. I was just standing there, minding my own business, when someone put their hands over my eyes. It made me jump and then I heard this deep, rich, brown voice.

"Hi, Jess, how you doing, girlfriend?"

I turned round. It was Janey. I hadn't seen her for ages. Yes, she was one of the many, but she lasted longer than the rest. We were together for nearly three whole months. I suppose you could call that a record for me — well since my four years with Sue at any rate.

"Janey, hi yourself." I grinned and gave her a big bear hug.

It was so good to see her. I don't know why we'd lost touch, probably laziness on my part. Maybe I thought she wouldn't want to know me after we broke up.

"So, girlfriend, why haven't you been in touch?" she asked, pretending to be really hurt.

"Not gonna lie to you, I'm just a lazy little shit," I said sheepishly. "Look, let me take these drinks over and I'll be back, then we can chat."

I took the tray over to the table and told the gang I'd be a minute.

Janey was ordering her drink when I got back to the bar.

"Are you on your own then?" I teased.

"I can't get serious about anyone else since you," she teased back.

"I've missed that."

"I'm waiting for some friends," she looked at her watch, "as usual I'm on time and they're late."

I told Janey we were here for a farewell drink for Katie. Janey had met all the gang except for her. We'd been split up a while when Katie came on the scene.

"She's gorgeous, has she got a girlfriend?" Janey asked looking over to the table.

What she said stunned me, as Janey's "gaydar" was notorious for being spot on. This time though she'd got it wrong, or had she?

"Kind of, she's married, to a man and about to go to New York with him. They're going to start a family," I said.

There must have been something in my voice as I could feel Janey looking at me.

"Have you got the hots for her?"

"No!"

"That means yes. Oh girlfriend, what have you got into?" Janey sounded concerned.

"It's nothing, I'll survive," I said. "Let's dance, I feel like letting off some steam."

I grabbed Janey's hand and dragged her to the dance floor.

We danced for a while before the music slowed down. I could see the rest of the gang do the come dancing routine and I also saw Katie heading for me.

"Janey, just follow my lead, I need you to help me get out of this," I said, just loud enough for her to hear.

"Okay, go for it," she said. I knew I could rely on her, even after all this time. I just hoped when she knew what I was going to do, she wouldn't back off.

I pulled her close and kissed her passionately. She didn't back away, but kissed me back. Suddenly I was pulled back in time, and all the old feelings I'd had for Janey returned. I managed to peer over her shoulder to see Katie's dejected look as she walked away. At least it'd worked. I released Janey but stayed within her arms as we held onto each other.

"Wow, Jess that was, well what can I say?" Janey was breathless.

I do have that effect when I kiss a woman. Yes, I know big head. But it's true, I am a brilliant kisser. Seriously, I've had no complaints.

"I'm sorry, I had an ulterior motive," I said sheepishly.

"Yeah, I realised that, but it was still great."

Janey didn't sound at all put out, which was a relief.

"Did Katie clock us then?"

"Yeah, she did, and I feel a right shit. But I had to do it. Things were getting out of hand."

"Come back to mine and tell me all about it," Janey said.

"What about your friends? Won't they wonder where you are?"

"It was a loose arrangement, so no worries. I'll text them."

"Okay, let's get out of here."

I went over to the table to let the others know I was going.

"Sorry about this guys but I'm gonna go. Janey and I've got some unfinished business," I said. I turned to Katie, who was not looking too happy with me.

"Have a good trip, Katie and enjoy New York."

I gave her a kiss on the cheek.

Josie gave me a funny look, but didn't say a word. I went back to Janey and we left for her place.

JANEY POURED TWO glasses of wine and joined me on the sofa. It was so nice being with her again. I'd missed her. She was great fun to be with.

So, why did I split with her if it was so good? Well, after the first flush of lust we realised it was just that, lust. We were going to be nothing but good friends. Mind you, seeing her again I wondered if we'd made a mistake as we were great in bed together.

I first met Janey at The Bird and we made a connection straight away. We had a real laugh together. She's such a beautiful woman, but that really doesn't do her justice. Her skin is a lovely honey brown, all soft and smooth. She has high cheekbones, so she'll never show her age. She keeps her hair cropped really short and has the head shape to carry it off. Janey has a body most women would die for, and at five feet eight looks like she ought to be on the catwalk. Boy did she look great, sexy as hell and my libido jumped into overdrive.

Janey turned and looked at me. She must have sensed how my hormones were now rushing around my body. She took my glass and put it with hers on the table then she leaned into me and we started kissing. What a kiss! I was getting horny as hell and could tell it was the same for Janey. She pulled away and got up, took my hand and led me to the bedroom.

"Are you sure about this?" I asked, as we were about to step into Janey's bedroom.

"I'm more than sure, girlfriend. Just get in there." She pushed me toward the bed.

I didn't need any more encouragement and before you could even say sex we were both as naked as the day we were born. Our eyes feasted on each other's naked bodies. I felt myself getting really wet and hard and reached out to touch Janey's breasts. Her nipples hardened in my palms and she moaned as I caressed them. She reached out and pulled me to her by my hips until one of her legs was between mine. I kissed her and our tongues danced. We rocked against each other's thighs until I could stand it no longer. I needed to be horizontal.

"Janey, I have to lie down before I fall down," I whispered in her ear.

She backed me up until the backs of my legs hit the edge of the bed and we fell onto it with her on top.

"Oh, baby, you want to be on top tonight?" I teased.

"No, I want you on top wearing the cock. I want you inside me filling me up."

God, I almost came there and then.

"Yeah, baby that sounds so good. Get it out now. I can't wait much longer."

Janey got off the bed and pulled the cock and harness out of the bedside cabinet drawer.

"I'll just go and wash this. I haven't used it for a while, I need to get the cobwebs off," she joked. "You get yourself hot for me."

I knew exactly what she meant as we used to do this a lot. She would go and wash the cock, even if it didn't need it, while I would let her come back and catch me pleasuring myself. It turned us both on even more than we already were. Sometimes it backfired and one of us would come before I'd even got the cock on. We both loved to watch while we made ourselves come. I would time it so that I was about to come as Janey got home from work. I would hear her key in the lock and start to moan loudly and know she was watching me through the crack in the door. This would turn me on even more and I'd come so hard I'd almost pass out. Then Janey would come in with her hand down her trousers and we'd have a great session.

My hand crept down to my clit, which was really hard and twitching madly. I covered it with my juices, and then I put my finger and thumb either side of it and started to jerk off as I waited for Janey to return. I looked up to see her watching me, her hand already between her legs, moving slowly as she rubbed her clit.

"I hope you're not too far gone," she said. "I want some action too."

"Plenty to last all night," I bragged.

She tossed the cock and harness over to me and I put it on while Janey lay on the bed and carried on rubbing her clit. God, she was really turning me on. I positioned the cock so it would stimulate my clit as I rode Janey. I got on the bed and lay on top of her and kissed her. She put her legs over the back of mine and I knew my cock was just at the entrance to her centre. I caressed her breasts as she grabbed my hips, urging me to enter her. She was obviously ready and didn't want to wait any longer. I braced myself on one hand and my knees. I held the cock and with Janey's help, pushed it into her. I felt her hips moving up to meet me and heard her sigh as I started to fill her deeply. I pulled out a little then back in slowly as she got used to the thickness. I moved in further each time and almost fully out before I would thrust in again. The feeling for me was exquisite and I knew it was good for Janey as I could see the look on her face and hear her moans.

"Oh, Jess that feels so good." Janey started to touch her clit to get a bigger orgasm out of me riding her with the cock. That really turned me on.

"Faster and harder baby, I'm gonna come soon." Her fingers were flying over her clit and I could feel my own clit twitching madly.

Needing no further encouragement, I started to increase my rhythm and as I did the pressure on my clit increased even more and I was ready to come as well.

"I'm gonna come too! Oh come with me baby," I said to Janey as I kissed her deeply.

"Oh yeah, baby. Now, I'm coming, now. Oh, baby it's so good yeah, oh yeah."

Janey thrust her hips to meet me and suddenly I felt the deep muscle spasms as my orgasm gathered and burst from me so powerfully that I swear I could see stars. I slowed my thrust to prolong the pleasure and to ensure Janey was satisfied. I gently pulled out from her and lay on my back grinning from ear to ear.

"Oh, babe, that was so fucking good," I said.

"Ditto to that, girlfriend, and now it's my turn." Janey reached to undo the harness.

Chapter Seven

I WOKE UP early with Janey curled up against me. She must have sensed I was awake and propping herself on one elbow kissed me on the cheek.

"Morning, girlfriend," she said, sleepily.

"Morning yourself."

"And don't you dare say it," she said, getting up and stretching. She was still naked and gave me a good view of her beautiful body. I lazily scanned it, but felt no arousal. Last night was what it was and really needed no explanation. I was aware of Janey waiting for an answer to her question.

"Say what?"

"It was good but it shouldn't have happened," she said, pulling her bathrobe on.

"I wasn't."

"But it's true, isn't it?"

I looked at her again. She was so gorgeous and I would have been lucky to have her as my girlfriend. But she wasn't Katie and I guess that's what she meant.

"I've got to be honest. Maybe we shouldn't have done it, but I really did enjoy it," I said, grinning like a teenager after the first time.

"Oh, yeah me too, but I felt as if you were somewhere else, with someone else."

"No, I wasn't thinking about anyone else but you."

Janey raised her eyebrows at me in an unspoken question. I sheepishly looked away as she'd caught me out trying to be chivalrous in sparing her feelings.

"You're right though, I wasn't totally here. But I really wasn't thinking about anyone else, I just wasn't as connected as before. I'm sorry." Now I was feeling bad.

"Nothing to be sorry for, we're adults and when I looked last night there were two of us. I could have said something. Jess, I was having so much fun and if I felt you were using me then I would have been really pissed. I guess I wanted to see if there was any chance for us and if we'd made a mistake splitting up."

Janey was one of the best. That's why we were going to be better at being friends.

"When we kissed in Nexus last night," I said, "I felt the old feelings come back and I suppose I was doing the same, wondering if we could make a go of it."

We looked at each other and grinned.

"Lust!" We said it together and laughed loudly.

"Well, at least we've sorted that out then. Let's get up. I'll cook breakfast and we can chat." She opened the bedroom door. "I'll shower first."

"Okay, sounds good to me, I'll join you," I teased.

"You can if you want. It'll save on water." She meant it too.

However, I waited until she finished before I went in.

By the time I got to the kitchen, Janey had cooked a full English breakfast with orange juice, coffee and toast. We talked as we ate.

"So, tell me about Katie, then," she said.

I told her all that had happened over the last few months, especially at the Murder Weekend. Telling her brought all the memories flooding back. How much I wanted Katie and how I'd resisted the temptation. She laughed when I told her about Josie's challenge.

"Well, girlfriend, you failed that one last night."

"No, no, no, I can discount that 'cos you're not a new conquest."

"Mmm, I don't think Josie would agree with you on that one." She grinned. "Katie is gay."

Her bold statement made me sit up and she saw my look of disbelief.

"Has the Janey gaydar ever been wrong?"

"Well no, I would say it's pretty well tuned in. Assuming your gaydar is right, what's she playing at?"

"Come on, Jess, she's not playing at anything. From what you've told me I'd say she's very confused. You and Katie have made a connection. She probably thought it would be okay to test her new feelings for women with you and you'd be all right with it being as how you're friends," Janey said. "Clearly that's not the case."

"Oh, right, I'm supposed to help every closet-dyke come out."

"No, not at all. I think she's under great pressure. You say she's a Catholic? That can be a problem in itself. Religion can really put a lot of pressure on you to follow the teachings of the Bible. Her parents will figure largely, especially if their faith is strong. Also there's pressure from society to live what's considered the normal," Janey did the quotation marks with her fingers, "life — husband and two point four children."

What was point four of a child anyway?

"Yeah, I guess what you've said is true. Trouble is I've let myself fall for her and I feel like I've been used."

"I know. I could tell you've let her get under your skin."

"Why can't she just admit who she is and—"

"And what, be with you for the rest of your lives?" Janey finished for me. "Katie's made her choice and you have to respect that. You have to try and get on with your life."

Harsh words, but what Janey said was true.

"I know. I thought it was hard getting over Sue, but this is gonna be worse," I said, tears beginning to course their way down my cheeks.

"Because you've fallen in love with her and she's the one." Janey knew how to get down to the nitty gritty of my problem. I had fallen in love with Katie and I guess until Janey verbalised it, I hadn't really given it any credence.

"Yeah, maybe subconsciously I've been fooling myself into thinking she would choose me over Bill and a move to New York," I said bitterly.

"Don't do that number on me, Jess. This is Janey. I could always see right through you."

"Sorry, why did I let so much time go by without getting in touch?" I asked, sad that I'd missed having Janey around.

"Probably because the time wasn't right until now, but you've never been out of my thoughts, you know. I expect it's been the same for you," she said.

"Yeah, I have thought about you."

"We don't have to be in each other's pockets to be friends."

She was right. We'd just slotted back in to our friendship without any problems. Okay, apart from sleeping together. At least we'd got past that, now we could have a good friendship without the obstacle of sex rearing its head.

"So, what do I do now?" I asked her.

"Well, how about coming on holiday with me? I've got friends in Toronto I haven't seen for over a year now. Come with me and have some fun. It'll do you good. You'll only need money for the flight, food and spending. What do you say?" Janey was full of enthusiasm.

Although it was a spur of the moment thing I had to agree it was a brilliant idea. I hadn't had a good holiday for a couple of years.

"Yeah why not, when?"

"I can't get away for a while. What about you?"

"I need to get some money together. I know I've got two weeks at the beginning of May," I said. Working for London Underground meant my holidays were mapped out for me.

"I think I can do May. I'll check when I get back to work and let you know. In the meantime I'll email Bev and Collette to see if the timing will be good for them and copy you in. Are you still using the same email address?"

"Yeah, although I may change it now. I don't want to be getting emails from Katie or I'll never get over her."

We chatted some more about going on holiday and then I left to go home. As I drove and thought about it, the more I liked the idea of going to Toronto. I've never been to America. Yes, I do know it's actually in Canada. My geography's bad, but not that bad. Now I'd got the chance to go. I would take it and enjoy myself. Janey had spoken loads of times about Bev and Collette and how nice they were. Now I'd get the chance to meet them. Maybe I'd also meet the woman of my dreams. Well, you never know. What is life if you can't dream?

It was obvious I had to accept Katie's decision to go and live the straight life. I knew it wasn't going to be easy for her. What if she met someone else and had to face that question yet again? What would she do? Would she spend the rest of her life never knowing what it was like to be with a woman, to make love to a woman? Never knowing how good it can be. Never being true to herself and having to hide her real feelings and always wondering, wondering. I knew some women who'd spent a long time before coming to terms with their sexuality. To me they'd wasted so much time. But then who am I to judge? I was lucky. I accepted it and got on with my life, not everyone's the same. How I wished Katie had the courage to take the first step in recognising who she is. It's so much easier now than it ever was in the past, but still women feel they can't be themselves.

At least I had the holiday to look forward to. I'd have to check my passport was in date.

I WAS OFF on Sunday so had a nice lie-in. I eventually roused myself, had a wonderful shower and then started a massive fry-up.

I was halfway through cooking when I heard a key in the lock. No, it wasn't someone breaking in. They wouldn't get much here. It was Josie. I gave her a spare set of keys after I locked myself out. Yes, I know that was stupid, but I bet you've done it too. Mind you, it won't happen a second time. I'd rather break in than get a locksmith out as it cost an arm and a leg. That was just to get in and then I had to pay to have all the locks changed. See what I mean? No one does it more than once.

"Hi, Josie," I shouted out. "You want breakfast?"

"Hi, Jess. Only if it's the full Monty. I'm in the mood for a big fry-up," she said as she came into the kitchen.

"I can assure you it's the works. Café Jess is now open."

Josie poured us both coffees as I continued cooking.

"I take it Katie and Bill got off all right," I said.

"Yeah, it was quite emotional. I'm really gonna miss her."

"We all will." I tried to keep my voice even.

"So, Janey's back then?"

I knew there had to be an ulterior motive. Josie doesn't often pop round unannounced.

"She's never been away," I said. "We just lost touch."

"Can I take it you failed the challenge then?"

"Yes, we did sleep together. It was a mistake, but a real fun one," I said and grinned.

"TMI, Jess."

"We split up because we couldn't make it as lovers. Thursday night just confirmed it. So we've decided to rekindle the friendship side of things"

"Ha! I knew you'd never do it."

"No, no. You can't count Janey, she's an old flame, not a new one."

"It's fine, I'm just teasing you." Josie grinned mischievously. "I figured you still had unfinished business on that score."

See, it's as I said before, she was a mind reader in a previous life.

"Yeah, I thought I still had feelings for her when we met on Thursday. I was wrong."

"So, now you've cleared that out of the way, you're going to be just good friends, are you?"

"Yeah, we're gonna be great friends." I smiled. "I'm so glad we met up again, I've really missed her. It wasn't until I saw her that I realised how much. I could kick myself for not keeping in touch."

"Don't beat yourself up over it. Your shifts don't help with keeping friendships going. Once you lose touch with someone it's surprising how much time goes past without you realising it," Josie said.

"Yeah, that's true. With our gang it's easy to keep in touch. I suppose with Janey it was the sex that probably made it hard for me to make the first move. We had to get over that before we could be friends. Now we have it's gonna be okay."

"I'm glad for you, Jess. Now perhaps you can get back to normal, whatever that is," Josie said and only just ducked the dishcloth I threw at her.

"Janey's invited me to go with her to Toronto. Her friends Bev and Collette live out there and she hasn't seen them for about a year," I said as I put the laden plates on the table.

"That'll be great, Jess. You haven't had a decent holiday for ages." Josie proceeded to tuck into the breakfast.

"I'm really looking forward to it. We'll stay with Bev and

Collette so it won't be too expensive," I said excitedly. "Still, who cares about the cost? I may never get another chance to go, so I'll make the most of it. Well, my credit card will."

"I always knew you and Janey would become good friends, eventually."

See, definitely a mind reader. Mind you, she's right about Janey and me. She is a good friend. Lovers come and go, but friends stay forever.

"When are you off to Toronto, then?"

"If we can arrange it, we're hoping to go the first two weeks in May. That's the earliest I can make it money-wise. Janey's going to let me know if she can get the time off. She's also got to check if it's okay with Bev and Collette. I hope so as I'm really looking forward to it."

"Well, if Janey can't get the time off, see if she can arrange it for you to go anyway. It would be good for you and you'd meet new people."

"Could do, I suppose."

It was a possibility, but hardly fair on Janey. She'd be so pissed off.

"Don't think you can forget the challenge while you're over there either. I shall have a word with Janey. I'm sure you'll have told her all about it."

I popped in the last mouthful of egg and bacon and put my knife and fork down with a satisfied sigh.

"Actually I wouldn't dream of forgetting the challenge. You were right, though I hate to admit it. I do need to sort myself out. I need to find someone special and maybe I will in Toronto. Who knows?"

"Now don't you go moving to the other side of the world as well. I couldn't bear that, both you and Katie so far away."

"Don't worry, Sis, I'll insist she moves over here." To be honest I couldn't be that far away from Josie. She's my little sister and I love her dearly. Since the death of our parents we'd become very close.

"Look at the time. I've got to go. Ivan and I are off to do some Christmas shopping," she said, looking at her watch.

"God, don't remind me. Give me an idea what I can get you and Ivan, please? I'm stumped at the moment."

We got up and Josie gave me a big hug. We walked arm in arm to the front door and I let her out.

"Don't worry about presents, just come to us for the day."

"Okay, I'd love to."

Josie got into her car and with a cheery wave drove back home. I waved back and then went to do the washing-up. Trust Josie to have to go shopping, leaving me with the clearing up. Ha, I'd get her back.

Christmas, it was only a couple of weeks away. God, how time flies when you're having fun.

WELL, CHRISTMAS AND New Year came and went. I did spend Christmas with Josie and Ivan and we had a great time. Janey went to her Mum's for the day and Boxing Day we spent together at mine. We became couch potatoes watching crap on the television and gorging ourselves on food. I'm sure I put on a stone over the Christmas and New Year period. I guess I'll have to renew my gym membership, at least for a couple of weeks. Actually, I quite enjoy going to the gym. Seriously, I do. It's a great place to check out the talent. Of course, I have an ulterior motive for going, doesn't everyone?

I didn't go out much over the next few months. I was saving up for the Toronto holiday. It's surprising how much you spend down the pub. As a group we go out quite a lot really, so the money I saved soon mounted up. It sounds like we're a load of heavy drinkers, but we're not really. So how often do we actually go out? Well, we meet up on Wednesdays at The Bird for a couple of hours and then most Saturdays to go to Nexus and sometimes the odd day during the week as well. Not everyone goes out every time; I work shifts so I don't. It's just great to chill out with your mates once in a while.

Chapter Eight

SO HERE I am getting packed and ready to go to Toronto. Janey spent the night here and Josie is going to take us to the airport. I do love my sister. It would've been murder trying to get the two of us plus our luggage on the train.

"Have you packed some warm clothes as well? It may be cold when we get there," Janey asked.

"Yeah, I haven't packed too much. I want to buy some new stuff over there."

"Ah, going to give your credit card a pasting eh?"

"Possibly, but I've got quite a bit saved so may not need to. I may not go again, so I'm gonna make the most of it."

I'd done a bit of overtime and hadn't gone out much so I'd got quite a nice little sum to go away with.

I put the last bits in the case and checked my list. I always make a list. It really helps. I started it about three weeks ago and it makes sure I don't forget anything. Yes right, I nearly always find there's something I've forgotten. Last time I went on holiday I forgot my camera. I had to buy those throwaway ones. It's not the same, but the pictures turned out quite well. This time I made sure I packed it first. I wasn't going to go all that way and take pictures on a throwaway camera.

"Right, passport, tickets, money, have I forgotten anything?" I muttered to myself.

"We're not going to the back of beyond, you know. They do have the odd shop if you've forgotten anything," Janey said.

"Sorry, I know I'm being a pain. It's been a long time since I went on holiday and I always seem to forget something. Mind you, as long as I've got my passport, the tickets and money, nothing else really matters."

"Very true," Janey said, as she lounged on the sofa watching me.

"Right, I'll just go and check all the windows." I got up from kneeling by my case.

"Relax, girlfriend, you're making me tired."

"Sorry. Josie's looking after the house so I'll leave it to her." I sat next to Janey. "Aren't you excited?" I asked her.

"Yeah, but it's too early in the morning to get that excited."

Just then I heard the key in the door.

"Hi, guys. I hope you're packed and ready to go." Josie's voice rang out as she came into the lounge.

"You're early," I said, looking at my watch. "We don't need to leave for another hour."

"I thought if you were ready, I'd buy you breakfast at the airport," she said.

"Sounds good to me. I'm ready," Janey said.

"Yeah me too, can you check the windows for me when you come back?" I asked Josie.

"Of course I will. Now let's get the car packed. I'm starving."

She picked up our hand luggage while we took our cases and trooped out to the car.

At that time of the morning the trip to the airport was quick and trouble free.

We were able to book in early and then went to get breakfast. We chatted about the trip and how much we were looking forward to getting away.

"This is from me and Ivan," Josie said, as she handed me some money.

I took it from her and saw it was fifty pounds.

"What's this for?"

"Call it an early birthday present. Buy something nice with it, or just blow it, as long as you enjoy yourself. You deserve it," she said.

I got up and hugged her.

"Thanks, Josie, you're the best. Give Ivan a big hug from me," I said, my eyes beginning to water.

We said goodbye at passport security and I told Josie I'd take lots of photos for her. I made a mental note to bring back something nice for her and Ivan.

THE FLIGHT WAS over seven hours long, which wasn't too bad, but still a bit tiring. There were a couple of films to watch, but most of the time we spent sleeping. Getting up early and being too excited to sleep much the night before was taking its toll. Hopefully jet lag wouldn't be too much of a problem.

Toronto is five hours behind the UK, so on the approach I changed my watch. It seemed funny to be arriving only three hours after we left Gatwick. I was now beginning to get nervous. Daft, I know, but I'd never met Bev and Collette. I'd seen pictures of them as Janey brought some over last night. They looked really nice and I was sure we'd get on, but it didn't quell my nerves.

Janey was now getting excited. She'd been pretty calm on the flight, but as we touched down she was fidgeting in her seat.

"Janey, calm down or I'll have to get the cabin staff to restrain you."

"I just can't wait to see them. It's been so long," she said.

At last the plane came to a halt and we disembarked. We weren't kept waiting long for our bags and soon we were on our way through customs.

Out in the arrivals lounge I saw two people waving frantically. It was Bev and Collette, I recognised them from the photos. Janey rushed forward and they all hugged. I stood back a bit and waited for Janey to introduce me.

"Jess, this is Bev and Collette," Janey said, at long last.

They both gave me a big hug and at once my nerves were gone. They were just how I imagined from the photos.

"Hi, Jess, welcome to Toronto," Bev said.

"Yeah, we hope you'll enjoy your stay," Collette said.

"I certainly will. I've been looking forward to this since Janey suggested it."

Once outside it wasn't as cold as I naively thought. It was nice and sunny, but a little bit chilly.

"It's not as cold as I thought it would be," I said.

"It can get extremely cold here in the winter, but it's warming up nicely now," Bev said.

"I must admit I did pack a couple of jumpers, just in case. But I travelled light as I want to hit the shops," I said.

"Shopping we can do lots of, if you want," Collette said. "There are some great shops in Toronto and we love it."

"I'm not really one for shopping, but it's different when you're on holiday," I said.

We packed our bags in the car and Bev drove out onto the highway.

"We live just outside Toronto and it'll take us about an hour and three quarters to get there," Collette said. "If you guys are tired, just sleep. We'll wake you when we're nearly there."

"No, I can't sleep now. I want to see everything. I've never been to Canada and I don't want to miss a thing." I was like a little kid in a toy shop at Christmas.

I watched the scenery as we left the confines of the airport. It started off very industrial, then countryside and suburban housing. Not much different from anywhere else, but still different, if you know what I mean.

I was so glad I'd decided to come away. I realised now how much I needed it.

I was still thinking about Katie more than I should, and I couldn't get her out of my mind for longer than a few hours. Maybe here in different surroundings I could start to purge her out of my system. I sound like I'm a computer. I went off into a world of my own on the drive. Janey, Bev and Collette were trying to catch up on more than a year of not seeing each other. I was sure they'd need more than the couple of weeks we'd got. Actually, it was sixteen days as we'd both managed to get extra time off. But even that wasn't going to be enough time for Janey.

The car went quiet, which brought me out of my reverie. I looked up and noticed we were driving alongside a river.

"Where are we?" I asked.

"That's the Niagara River," Collette said, and she looked at Janey and gave her a conspiratorial wink.

Suddenly we rounded a curve and I saw what could only be Niagara Falls!

"Oh my God, it's amazing. You didn't tell me we were coming to Niagara," I said to Janey.

"I wanted to surprise you."

"You've certainly done that," I said.

Janey took a picture of me.

"Why are you taking my picture?"

"Your face is a picture and I promised Josie I'd record it for her."

Bev and Collette were laughing.

"Your face really was a picture," Collette said.

"It was indeed. I hope Janey caught it right," Bev said.

"Josie knew? Are you all in on it?"

"Yep," Bev said.

"Well, it's a great surprise and I can't wait to go and see it up close and personal." I grinned back at them like a Cheshire cat. I couldn't take my eyes off it.

"I think food and rest is in order. You've got plenty of time to explore," Collette said.

"True and I am feeling a bit tired," I said.

"Lightweight," Janey said, as she nudged me in the ribs. "Don't tell me you're not tired."

"Well—"

"We'll see," I said.

"This is the Niagara Parkway, and as you can see it caters for the tourists," Bev said, acting as tour guide.

I could see what she meant. There were more B & B's than you could shake a stick at.

Bev and Collette's house was just off the Niagara Parkway. We turned onto the drive of a massive detached house.

"My God, it's bigger than I expected," I said. Then realised how that must sound. "Sorry, I didn't mean to be rude."

"Not at all," Bev said. "It used to be a B & B but was extremely run down so we got it real cheap."

"I had some money left to me by an old spinster aunt," Collette added. "We'd saved a bit and only needed a medium-sized mortgage to get it done up."

"You should have seen it when they first got it," Janey said.

"It was in a bit of a state," Bev agreed.

"That's an understatement. There was only one habitable room. We all had to bunk down in a caravan until we got it liveable," Janey said.

Collette laughed. "Yeah, poor Janey came over for a month's holiday and ended up working her butt off."

"It must have been fun though, seeing it take shape. Look what you've got now, it's beautiful," I said.

"Thank you, we love it," Bev said, as she popped the boot or trunk as the Canadians call it over here.

We got the bags out of the car and trooped inside. It was lovely and warm not only because of the heating, but the way it was laid out and decorated. God, I sound like an estate agent. On the left we have the kitchen. Actually, it was on the right. We dumped the bags in the hall and took off our jackets before going into it.

"The good thing about this house is all four bedrooms have bathrooms. So there's no queuing in the morning," Collette said. "There were originally six bedrooms of average size but only three had their own bath and there was a communal bath for the others."

"We weren't keen on that so we remodelled and ended up with four large bedrooms all with their own bath," Bev said.

"Yeah, buying an old B & B does have its advantages," Bev agreed.

I smelled the coffee and could see the table laid out for the four of us. It was a huge pine table and had six very heavy pine chairs set out around it. We sat down and Bev poured the coffee.

"Right, what have you guys eaten?" She asked.

"We had breakfast at Gatwick and then the usual airline food," I said.

"And you know what that's like, so now I'm starving," Janey said, with feeling.

"Me too," I said.

"Okay, we got steak and salad, how does that sound?" Collette asked.

"Sounds like a feast for a king," I answered.

"Right, we'll start cooking while you freshen up. Your bedroom is top of the stairs, first door on the left. I take it you don't mind sharing?" Collette asked.

"Not at all, I can just about put up with Jess' snoring," Janey said.

"Hey, I don't snore, you cheeky sod." I jabbed Janey in the ribs.

"Girlfriend, you snore enough to wake the dead," she said, moving away so as not to get another dig. "Actually, she doesn't make a sound. One night she was so quiet I thought she'd died. I had to shake her awake to make sure she was still alive."

It was true. I remember being rudely awoken during our dating days. I'd sat up, looked at Janey, told her to fuck off and went promptly back to sleep. We laughed about it the next morning.

"Well, I'm glad you two get along all right," Bev said laughing. "You were right, Janey, you two are better as friends."

I jumped back in mock horror. "Friends, who said we're friends? I've never seen this woman before in my life. She just followed me onto the plane."

We fell about laughing. The ice was completely broken and I could relax. I'm not good at meeting people for the first time, but Bev and Collette were great, my kind of people. They would really get on with the gang back home and I made a mental note to return the compliment of hospitality.

Isn't it strange how you can feel comfortable with some people straight away? Others you could spend a lifetime with and never ever feel you know them or get comfortable with them. It's a bit like the instant attraction you get for someone you fancy. Only this is to do with friendship, if you know what I mean.

Janey and I went up to the bedroom. It was as large as Bev had said, with a beautiful en suite bathroom including a shower. There was only one bed but it was a king size and I knew it wouldn't worry us. We knew we could sleep together and actually sleep.

Janey threw herself on the bed.

"Don't lay there, you won't want to get up," I said, going into the bathroom to splash cold water on my face. I was beginning to feel quite tired now.

"I'm too excited to, there's so much to see and do. The last time I was here I was working on this place and I didn't get much chance to go out. It'll be so much fun showing you the places I've been to."

"How many times have you been over here?" I asked.

"Only three times, the last was about eighteen months ago. That was when I got roped into working on the refurbishment," she said. "It was great fun, but tiring."

"How come you've never mentioned it before?"

"I have. You just never took it in I guess."

I thought back to the time we were together. I vaguely remember Janey talking about Bev and Collette, and she must have mentioned Canada, but it obviously didn't register.

"We'll go on the Maid of the Mist and up to the Casino. Oh, there are loads of things I want to show you." Janey sounded excited.

I knew how she felt, just being here was exciting. Once I'd washed my face I felt better. I jumped on the bed with Janey and gave her a cuddle.

"What's that for, girlfriend?"

"Just my way of saying thanks for inviting me to come with you. I wouldn't have missed this for the world and it'll certainly do me good and recharge my batteries. Niagara Falls, who'd have thought I would actually be here."

"I'm glad you're here too. Bev and Collette have only got a few days off and I need someone to go out with." Janey loved to tease me.

"True and you know no one else would put up with you."

I ran out of the room to avoid the pillow she heaved at me.

We had an early dinner and talked about what we'd do. As we were tired, it was decided we'd stay at home talking and chilling, anything else would be wasted on us. It was fine by me as it gave me a chance to get to know Bev and Collette.

They had the weekend off and also managed to get a couple of extra days off as well, so they could take us out and show us the sights.

Bev and Collette told us they had some friends coming from New York on our last weekend. It was a long-standing arrangement that they didn't want to break. There was a good chance they were bringing a friend hence the reason we were bunking in together. It saved moving when they arrived.

"I hope you guys are okay with it. Becki and Sydney are a great couple and I'm sure you'll get on with them," Collette said.

"Sounds great," Janey said.

"Does it take long to get to New York?" I asked.

"About an hour or so. It's great if you want to do a bit of shopping," Bev said. "Are you thinking of going there then?" Collette asked.

"It's a thought. What do you reckon, Janey? Do you fancy a trip to New York?" I asked.

"Why not, if we've got time to fit it in."

"Right, just a few rules before we forget," Bev said.

She clocked the looks on Janey's face and mine and cracked up laughing.

"Ha, that got you. Seriously, since we're gonna spend a lot of time together we need to make it workable. Your bedroom and bathroom is your responsibility, but the rest of the house is where we all pitch in together. The same goes for the cooking."

"Sounds fine to me. I didn't expect maid service. I do a mean roast beef and Yorkshire pudding, I'd love to cook for you both. Janey's already sampled my cooking and survived to tell the tale," I chimed in.

"Great, the only other thing is food. I think if we start with fifty dollars each we should be okay. We can top it up as and when," Collette said. "If we put it in this bowl and any time we buy anything we just take the money out."

"Brilliant, that saves having to work out who owes what to whom," Janey said.

Once we'd sorted out the domestic arrangements, we had coffee and relaxed in the room warmed by a roaring log fire.

The rest of the day was spent getting to know each other better. Actually it was more about me getting to know Bev and Collette. I really bonded with them both and felt it was reciprocated. They were so easy-going that it was strange to think I'd only known them a few hours. The conversation never flagged and it was so comfortable being with them.

AFTER WE'D EATEN we went for a walk and they showed us the immediate surroundings. It was really beautiful and I felt I could stay forever. But that's holidays for you. They give you a false sense of what it would be like to move to wherever you were. Trouble is that holidays never last. Very soon reality sets in and you realise you still have to work to live, unless of course you're loaded. I've seen all the programmes on television about people moving abroad. Good luck to them. I still prefer England, though I could definitely get a feel for Canada.

We settled back indoors and I felt the tiredness creep up on me as I yawned. I looked at my watch. It was only just after seven, but we'd been up since seven o'clock English time.

"If you want to go to bed early, just go. We don't stand on ceremony in this house. Just do what you would at home," Bev said.

"Thanks, I think I will go up and see how long I can sleep for," I said, stifling another yawn.

"Go for it girl, and if you wake in the night just help yourself to food or coffee or whatever. There's plenty of books on the shelves, as you can see, to help you get through the night," Collette said.

"I'm gonna stay up a bit longer. Lots to catch up on," Janey said.

She looked tired too, but I guess she was fighting it so she could catch up with her friends. It was understandable, as she hadn't seen them for over a year.

"No worries. I'll see you all in the morning," I said and made my weary way to bed.

God was I tired. Hopefully we'd timed the flight well and would be able to get over the jet lag quickly. I didn't want it to spoil our time here. Maybe we could go to a gay club and I'd meet someone nice. At least I hadn't thought of Katie for a whole day. Now that was progress indeed. Then I started to think about her, another step back then. I knew it would take time, but it's been nearly six months since she went to New York. Just an hour or so by plane from here that is. No, don't worry I'm not going to try and bump into her. That wouldn't do either of us any good at all.

It was getting better even though I was reluctant to admit it. But I wasn't sure I wanted to get over Katie. It was almost as if I wanted to be pining over her. How sad is that? I obviously didn't want to let her go. Maybe it was a case of I'd put her on the back burner, as Mel would say, because of getting organised for the holiday. Now I'd got time to think, she came to the front, but it was too painful to deal with. If I just put it away, I could pretend it was dealt with and just ignore it. Does that make sense? Oh, I'm so glad you understand it. Can you explain it to me please? Now I've started to think about her and the fact that she's not far away, I realise I miss her like crazy. Yet I know I couldn't have dealt with just having her friendship. If you'd tasted her kisses you'd know what I mean.

I undressed and climbed into the king size bed, which was lovely, warm and comfy.

"WAKE UP LAZY bones." Janey was shaking me.

I forced my eyes open.

"What time is it?"

"Nearly midday," she replied.

"God, I must've slept like the dead. I feel better for it though."

"Bev and Collette are up, I can hear them downstairs. Come on, let's get some breakfast. I'm starving."

I could see Janey was already dressed. Didn't jet lag affect her?

"How can you be so bright?" I asked.

"Oh, I still feel tired, but I'm fighting it. Come on, girlfriend, get showered and I'll see you downstairs."

I stood in the shower letting the water wash the tiredness away. I felt so much better, and as I got dressed I felt almost human.

After breakfast we went for a walk alongside the Niagara River. We found a nice restaurant and had lunch. The food was great and it wasn't that expensive.

In the evening we went to a gay bar in Toronto where they had line dancing. I'd never done anything like that and had a great time. They did bar meals, so we didn't have to worry about going home to eat. By the time we got back I was really tired and could see Janey was also feeling the strain.

We sat in the lounge having a nightcap before we went to bed, talking about what to do the next day. There was such a lot to do and see, it was going to be hard to fit it all in.

Chapter Nine

"WHAT TIME DO Becki and Sidney land tomorrow?" I asked.

I could hardly believe we only had four full days left before we went back on Sunday. The time had gone by in a flash and there were still lots of things to see and do. At least I would have an excuse to come back.

"Five o'clock, so we need to leave here just after three to get there in time," Collette said.

"You guys gonna come with us?" Bev asked.

"Yeah, what say I do a nice beef stew for dinner?" I asked.

They'd sampled my roast and were very impressed. They seemed to enjoy my basic English food. Either that or they were just being kind.

"Great, it'll be nice to have something warming when we get back," Bev said.

"I'll even do some dumplings and maybe make an apple crumble for sweet," I said.

"Wow that sounds wonderful. Are you trying to fatten us all up?" Janey asked, with a laugh.

"No, I just fancy having a pig out."

I spent the morning preparing and cooking the stew, which I would leave to cool once it was done. It always tastes better when all the ingredients have had time to marinade together. Tomorrow, when we got back from the airport, I would heat it up and add the dumplings. I could also prepare the crumble mix and store it in the fridge. That way it wouldn't take long to do dinner the next day and I wouldn't miss any of the conversation. I wasn't too worried about meeting Sidney and Becki as Bev and Collette had made me feel so welcome.

COLLETTE CHECKED WITH the airport before we left to make sure the flight was on schedule. We set out in plenty of time and arrived without encountering too much traffic. I was getting used to being on the wrong side of the road as Bev had let me drive a couple of times. Her car was quite small and easy to drive. Collette had an SUV and was very protective of it. She didn't even let Bev drive it. I think it was because she'd only had it a few months and she was still enjoying the newness of it. We took the SUV as there were going to be six of us to transport. Collette navigated her way into the car park and found a space near the entrance to the airport. While we stood waiting for Becki and Sidney we were chatting and checking out the talent. There were some really hot women travelling and we played the game of—is she or isn't she—to pass the time away.

"They're in the baggage hall," Collette said, looking at the monitor. "They shouldn't be too much longer now."

"Great, I was gonna get us some coffee, but we can wait 'til we get back," Bev said.

It was only a short time and suddenly there were loads of people flooding out the arrivals exit. I'd seen pictures of Becki and Sidney so looked intently at the faces coming toward me. Then I spotted someone I never expected to. It was Katie. She hadn't seen me yet so I had time to compose myself. She was with two other women, and as I looked I realised it was Becki and Sidney. Is this the biggest coincidence or a great slap in the face from the payback god?

"Over here, you two," Bev shouted, nearly deafening me as she was standing so close.

"Hi, you guys." Becki grabbed Bev and Collette and gave them both a big hug.

Then Sidney joined in and it became a massive group hug.

I looked at Janey who had just clocked Katie and turned to look at me.

"Is that who I think it is?" She whispered in my ear.

It was all I could do to nod.

"After much persuasion Katie decided to come with us," Becki said.

"Great, the more the merrier," Collette said.

"Katie's, just moved here from England. Katie, these are our good friends Bev and Collette," Becki said, doing the introductions.

"Hi, Katie, you're very welcome," Bev said. "This is Janey and Jess. They're also from England."

"Hi, Janey, Jess and I know each other from London," Katie said, giving me one of her smiles.

I tried not to show how much it was affecting me.

"Oh that's good, at least you know three people now. You'll get to know the rest of us very soon." Collette led the way to the car park.

I held back with Janey.

"Jesus, that's a shocker," I said, just loud enough for her to hear as we followed the rest.

"Got to be the biggest coincidence I've ever heard of," Janey replied. "How do you feel about spending the next three days with her?"

"Gonna be hard, I don't mind admitting. But it won't spoil what's left of the holiday."

"Don't worry, girlfriend, I've got your back," Janey teased.

"You'd better have, trust this to happen just when I was getting over her."

"No you weren't, so don't try and pretend you were."

Janey knows me too well.

"All right, so I wasn't getting over her as quickly as I thought, but I still don't need this," I said.

"Come on you two, stop dawdling," Bev said.

We caught up and sat at the back of the SUV, letting Becki and Sidney sit close to Bev and Collette so they could chat. Katie sat with Becki and Sidney. I was able to look at the back of her head and send her leave me alone vibes. I was really glad Janey was with me. At least I could use her help not to make a prat of myself. I wondered how much Katie had confided to Becki and Sidney. Did they know what had happened on the Murder Weekend? When we got back I'd try and get a chance to chat with Janey and ask her how to play it. It occurred to me that now I wanted the time to go quickly with Katie on the scene. This weekend was going to be a long one, that's for sure.

I'd put the oven timer to start half an hour before we got in so all I had to do was to prepare the dumplings. I got Janey to help so I could chat to her. I gave her the job of getting the apples partly cooked ready for the crumble in the fridge to go on top and then I would put it in the oven while we ate the stew. The others went into the lounge and let us get on with it.

"Janey, what the hell am I going to do?"

"Hey, girlfriend, there's nothing to do. You just behave normally and get on with Katie as best you can."

"How much do you think she's told Becki and Sidney?"

"Knowing how much we girls talk when we're together, I guess the whole lot."

I knew she was right. We girls love to confide in each other. Now, how much of a fool did I feel? People I'd never met before knowing so much about me.

"Yeah, I expect you're right," I said.

"Look, don't get worried about it. You've got to remember, Katie never thought this would happen. Come on, Jess, how bizarre is it?" Janey said, laughing. "She moves to New York, pals up with lesbians and probably tells them all about you and her. Those said lesbians have friends in Canada, who, just happen to be friends with me, who happens to be friends with you. Let's face it you couldn't make it up."

"Yeah, it is bizarre. I'd never have believed it if it hadn't happened to me." I grinned at the absurdity of life and all its little quirks.

"The trick is to duck when life throws you the odd curve ball. You've got to take this in your stride. I think Katie will get the idea that you and I are together, especially when she knows the sleeping arrangements. Now, it's up to you how far you let that idea settle in her head," Janey said, a little too mischievously.

"Right." I can be a little dense sometimes. I hadn't thought about that one. I guess I was too close to the problem. "If I let her think we're together, it will make this weekend go a little smoother."

If I played it the way Janey was suggesting, Katie would get the message that she should not try to recreate the Murder Weekend situation.

"At least if she thinks we're together, she won't try anything. I know she's been hurt in the past by fellas who've played away, so she won't do the same."

"Didn't stop her last time," Janey reminded me.

"True. Oh, I don't know any more, I just wish she wasn't here now," I bemoaned, giving the stew a stir before adding the dumplings. I put potatoes on to boil and some green beans.

"Don't worry, just let's make sure the next couple of days are fun no matter what."

"Absolutely. I promise I won't do anything to spoil the rest of the holiday," I said.

"RIGHT, GUYS, ARE you all up for a bit of line dancing?" Bev asked, after we'd had lunch.

"You bet," Sidney said.

"Sounds good to me," I said. I really enjoyed the last time and was keen to go again.

"I've never done it before, but I'm willing to give it a go," Katie said.

"Okay, we'll go to Pink Peacocks. I think they've got a special on tonight. There'll be lots of food so no cooking for any of us tonight," Bev said.

"I guess you're all right going to gay clubs?" Collette asked Katie.

"Yeah, I used to go all the time in England," Katie said. "And I've been out with Becki and Sydney in New York so I think you could call me a veteran."

"I just wanted to make sure you wouldn't be uncomfortable in a gay club," Collette said.

"The only problem is I feel the odd one out, being the only

straight one here," she said.

"That's fine, honey, we'll make you an honorary lesbian for the next couple of days," Sidney said.

"It means you'll have to kiss the door woman to get in, just like all good lesbians though," Bev said with a straight face.

"Oh yes, of course," Katie said not sure how to take Bev's remark.

"Take no notice, she's only kidding," Collette said giving Bev a sharp dig in the ribs.

Everyone laughed as Bev pretended to double up in pain.

We got to the club and found a good spot right by the dance floor and close to the bar. Everyone looked great in their cowboy gear. I was so glad we'd gone shopping and I'd got some bits that were suitable. I'd splashed out on some decent boots with the intention of carrying on the dancing when I got back home. I was really enjoying myself. We all got up for the dances and hardly sat down at all. It wasn't all line dancing, there were times when we could dance with partners. It was very well done, as there were a couple of women who were showing everyone what to do. It meant that newcomers, like me, were able to learn more dances.

Janey and I got up a few times to whirl round the dance-floor and I was getting quite good at the steps. I had to lead though, as I was absolutely hopeless going backwards. I have to see where I'm going, otherwise I fall over. I don't mind falling over when I've had a few too many, but not stone cold sober. Well, actually, I do mind, it bloody well hurts and I feel such a fool.

Katie was behaving herself and not giving me the eye the way she had in England. She was really good at the cowboy two-step. She and Becki certainly looked expert as they danced. Was I jealous? Nah. Well, maybe just a little. There were a lot of really good-looking women here and my ideal woman could be somewhere among them. No, I still thought of Katie that way. I really must stop thinking like that. Maybe I should stop thinking, period.

While Katie was here I couldn't pick someone up. I'd feel like I was betraying her somehow. Is that stupid or what?

"Do you want to dance?" Katie stood at my side and held her hand out to me.

I didn't like to say no as it might've looked a little odd. Besides, I did want to dance. Not just because Katie had asked me, but because I was enjoying myself. I was, really.

"Yeah sure," I said, as I got up.

It was the cowboy two-step, which I was now quite adept at.

We held each other and I did a mental count to get us moving. Sounds very technical, but I was still trying to get used to it and having Katie in my arms would definitely put me off my stride if I didn't.

It felt good holding Katie again. It did mean, of course, that I was setting myself back a few steps regarding getting over her. But hey, what the heck. Just have fun, Jess.

"Is this a coincidence or what?" She asked as we danced.

"I'd never have believed it if someone told me," I said. "How are things in the Big Apple?"

I wanted to keep the topic of conversation general as I didn't want her to start talking about us.

"It was hard at first with not working, although I have sent out my CV in the hope that Bill will let me go out to work. In the meantime, because I was getting bored staring at four walls, I enrolled in keep fit classes and met Becki. She's really great."

"Yeah, she seems nice," I said.

"It's funny how I pal up with a couple of lesbians."

My instant thought was—like drawn to like—and I mentally kicked myself for being so bitchy.

"Just like being in England, eh?"

"Yeah but not the same. I miss you guys so much." Katie sounded sad as she said that.

"Well, I'm sure you'll be back to visit your family, we can all get together then."

"True. I hope to fix up a visit in the next few months. I'll let Josie know and she can tell everyone else." She moved in and held me a little closer. Remind you of something? Yes, the dance floor incident all over again.

I know I should have released my hold, but I didn't. I was enjoying it too much and didn't care who saw. At least I didn't have to keep an eye out for Josie. Then I remembered I was supposed to be with Janey and pulled away to a respectable distance.

"Sorry," Katie said.

We finished the dance, Katie went back to the table and I went to the bar to get a round of drinks in.

"You and Katie look good together," Janey said, as she came to help me.

"Yeah, but it's not gonna happen, is it?" I turned to her as I spoke. "Why did she have to come with them? Couldn't she have stayed at home like the dutiful little wife and leave me alone?"

"Well, she hasn't actually done anything, has she?"

"Yeah, she's got back under my skin," I said.

"No she hasn't. She never left, did she?"

"Let's get the drinks back to the table." I wasn't going to admit Janey was right.

I sat sipping my beer and told myself to get it together and enjoy the evening. It was silly to let this spoil what was otherwise a great night out. It was a line dance next and we all got up to join in. It was quite complicated and I tripped over my own feet more than once. I ended up laughing so much I had to leave the dance-floor for a while. I stood watching and checking out the steps, then joined back in with much more success.

By the time we got back I was knackered. I hadn't danced so much in a long time. We sat in the lounge talking and drinking until the early hours and I couldn't see anyone getting up to cook breakfast before noon.

SUDDENLY IT WAS Sunday, the day we were due to fly back to London. It was too soon as it felt like we'd only just arrived. I really didn't want to leave. I could have stayed forever, but all good things have to come to an end.

"Right everyone, listen up." Collette grabbed our attention at breakfast. "Janey and Jess, your flight is at ten this evening. Becki, you guys take off an hour before that. So, I think we should all go in time for the nine o'clock flight, take up residence in the bar and wait for the second one."

"It's a plan," Bev said.

"Bet your ass it is." Sidney grinned.

Bev pretended to be upset. "All right there's no need to mock."

"What time do we need to leave?" I asked. I still had a few things left to pack.

"About six should give us plenty of leeway," Collette replied. She was going to drive us.

"Great, that gives me time to go out for a last look at Niagara Falls, and then I'll come back to finish my packing," I said, getting up.

"It's all right. You can come back to visit you know, and you don't have to come with Janey. You're our friend as well now," Bev said, laughing.

"Thanks, that'd be great." I went out for a short walk before we left as I still had some pictures I wanted to take. I had to show the guys back home where I stayed and the surrounding area. I snapped away for about an hour and made my way reluctantly back to the house. When I got back I finished my packing. Finally, I was ready so I took my bags downstairs to find the others waiting.

"Sorry, am I late?"

"No, we were just ready early. Well, we might as well get the car packed and leave."

We left right on time and had a good drive to the airport. After we checked our bags in we went to the bar to wait for the first flight.

"Well, I've had a really great time and will be back to bother you before you know it," I said to Bev and Collette.

"You're more than welcome. We've enjoyed your company," Bev said.

"It was great meeting you guys too," I said, as I turned to Becki and Sidney. "It's nice to know Katie has made a couple of good friends over here."

"Why, thank you," Becki said. "Katie is lucky to have you and your friends to look out for her."

"We're a big happy bunch at home and do care about each other," I said, looking at Katie and then the rest of them.

"We all miss you, Katie, but at least I can tell the guys at home you're doing well. They'll never believe we actually met up," I said, laughing at the coincidence of it.

"It's all right. I'll send Josie an email to prove it," Katie said, joining in the laughter.

The flight for New York was called and we got up to go to the gate to say our goodbyes.

I said goodbye to Becki and Sidney and gave them both a hug.

"Now you've met us too, don't be a stranger. You're more than welcome to come and visit with us in New York," Sidney said.

"Yeah, it'll give you a chance to touch base with Katie as well," Becki said.

"Thanks, I'd love to. I wanted to go to New York to do some shopping, but we couldn't fit it in this time."

"Bye, Jess, give my love to everyone back home," Katie said, as she gave me a hug.

I held on a bit longer than I should have, I just didn't want to let go. I knew it would be a long time before I'd see her again. Next time we met up I hoped to be over her. So I wanted to say a proper goodbye now with a big hug. Shame I couldn't give her a proper kiss as well.

"I will. Next time I come over you'll have to show me New York," I said, trying to sound cheerful.

"I'd love to."

"Come on, we'll miss the plane." Becki chivvied Katie along.

We stood waving until they'd disappeared.

I went to the rest rooms while the others went back to the bar to wait for our flight to be called. When I got back the three of them were deep in conversation.

"Hi, what are you guys talking about?" I asked.

"Just deciding when we're going to come over to England," Bev replied.

"Oh, great, when will you be able to get over?"

"Hopefully next fall," Collette said.

"That's autumn to you," Janey said.

"I'm not a complete moron, you know." I gave Janey my best 'you're in trouble' stare.

We chatted about Bev and Collette coming over. They'd probably stay most of the time with Janey, but maybe they could fit in a couple of days with me as well.

Chapter Ten

I FELT QUITE deflated on the journey home and I put that down to the holiday being over and seeing Katie. Which made me start thinking about her again. Like I said before, I'd put her on the back burner and not dealt with the whole situation. I closed my eyes and listened to the hum of the engines. I was going to have to stop feeling sorry myself, I knew that. But, that was easier said than done. When we get back I'll have a chat with Janey, she'll have some words of wisdom, I'm sure. I'd always been able to talk to Janey and was glad she was back in my life. Not just so I could talk to her about Katie. Of course not. Maybe I needed someone to take me in hand to put me on the straight — metaphorically speaking — and narrow. She could definitely be relied upon to do that.

Janey was staying with me until we both went back to work on Thursday, so it would give us time to talk. We'd also planned to go to Brighton for one of the days. I love Brighton. It's great to walk along the sea front this time of year, get a beer in one of the promenade bars and just chill. There were slightly less people as well, which made it great for shopping. Yes, I know I said I'm not a great shopper, but I have periods when I quite enjoy it, especially in the little shops in Brighton. Then I can shop 'til I drop.

I must have drifted off to sleep, because the next thing I knew was Janey shaking me.

"Come on, girlfriend, we're about to land." She tightened her seat belt.

"Great, I slept through the whole flight," I said, yawning and trying to stretch in the confines of what little space there was.

"Yeah, and you were snoring."

"Never, you said I don't snore."

"Not when you're in bed, no, but slumped in an air-plane seat, yes," Janey said laughing. "I was just glad I had the head-phones on to watch the movie."

"Then how did you know I was snoring?"

"I could hear it 'til I turned the sound up."

Then I knew she was joking.

"Yeah, right." I bumped her shoulder.

We collected our bags and got through customs with no problems. I must admit I did have a bit more than I should have, so I was glad we didn't get stopped. Well, it was only an extra two hundred cigs for one of the guys at work and an extra bottle of my favourite perfume.

I told Josie we'd get a taxi back, as it was a ten in the morning arrival. It would save her trying to get time off work to pick us up. When the taxi pulled up outside my house, Josie's car was parked there. I hoped nothing was wrong. We paid the driver, took our bags inside and left them in the lounge and went in search of my little sister.

"Hi, you two, did you have a good time?" Josie's voice rang out from the kitchen and so we went and joined her.

"It was absolutely brilliant," I said, giving her a big hug.

"Good, I'm glad. I decided to take today off anyway and get you some breakfast. I've also done a roast beef for you to heat up later." She looked bemused as both Janey and I laughed. "What?"

"We did a roast for the guys in Canada," I said.

"Yeah, and a stew with dumplings for when Becki, Sidney and Katie came from New York for our last weekend," Janey added.

"Katie?"

"She's friends with Becki and Sidney who are friends with Bev and Collette."

Josie thought we were kidding. "I don't believe it."

I went to the lounge and brought my laptop into the kitchen. I took the photo card from my digital camera, put it in the laptop and brought up all the pictures we'd taken. Don't you just love computers?

"Here, have a look, the camera doesn't lie," I said, getting her to sit at the table. "Janey, you can explain. I really need the loo," I said, leaving them to it.

"You and Katie look very cosy," Josie said, when I returned.

I looked over her shoulder and there was a picture of me and Katie dancing the cowboy two-step. Shit! Who took that? I looked at Janey who had the good grace to look away sheepishly.

"That was when we went line-dancing. It was a great night. Katie dragged me up to do the cowboy two-step," I said, hoping I sounded more normal than I felt.

Just looking at the picture brought the memories of that dance flooding back, and how good it felt to hold her in my arms again. I must admit, looking at it, if I was Josie I'd have got the wrong impression.

"Line-dancing. That sounds like fun." I was wrong, she didn't get the wrong impression or if she did, she hid it well.

"It is," Janey said. "I'd always thought it was a nerd's thing. When I tried it though, it was great, I really enjoyed it."

Janey was trying hard.

"Look, I was thinking of going to a local line-dancing club. Will you come with me," I asked Josie, "cos I don't fancy going alone, not the first time?"

"I must admit, I've always wanted to have a go myself," Josie said. "Yeah, I'll come with you. I wouldn't want to go on my own the first time either."

At least it got her off the picture of Katie and me. I clicked the next picture and we got through about half of them before we had a late breakfast. I was really glad of the break. Not only was I hungry, but also it gave us a chance to get onto a different topic. We still stayed with Katie, but at least not me and Katie.

"How is Katie getting on really?" Josie asked. "She sounds as if she's having a good time, but — "

"She's doing fine, but she said it was hard to meet people and make friends, mainly because she's not working. She met Becki at a keep-fit class."

"I think she's working on Bill to let her go back to work," Janey added.

"That's right. She told me she's put her CV out to the agencies."

"I don't know why he's hung up on her not going out to work," Josie said.

"It's 'cos he's a control freak. He wants her at his beck and call," I said angrily. "Doesn't he know we're in the twenty-first century now?"

"Oh come on. He's not that bad," Josie said.

"So why won't he let her go out to work?"

"In her emails she said he wants her to settle in a bit first," Josie said.

"Look guys, it's none of our business at the end of the day," Janey said.

She was right, as usual.

"True," I said.

"All right, point taken," Josie said, clearing the plates.

"Now we've eaten 'til bursting point, let me get the present I got for you, Josie," I said, going to the lounge to get it out of my bag.

I handed her a small box, neatly wrapped. No, I didn't do it. I'm crap at that sort of thing. I just hoped she'd like it.

"Oh, Jess, it's lovely." She took the delicate necklace out of the box.

"We went to one of those little arts and crafts fairs. I saw this and thought of you straight away," I said, pleased she liked it.

"It's perfect, thank you." She had tears in her eyes and gave me a great big hug.

"Steady on, you'll have me in tears too," I said, laughing. "I got Ivan some cufflinks in the same design, only more masculine."

"Let me see?"

"No, you'll have to wait 'til he opens it. I spent ages wrapping them," I said straight-faced.

"Yeah, and I'm a drag queen," she said, laughing.

"Well—"

"Don't even go there," Josie said. "So you're in the wrapping business now?" She said turning to Janey.

Janey grinned. "Guilty as charged. You recognised my technique?"

"No, I just knew Jess wouldn't do it herself and wouldn't pay to get it done."

"Oh, I am so wounded," I said.

"Look, I'm gonna leave you to unpack and I can get back home to Ivan," Josie said, getting her coat and bag.

"You should have invited him over to share with us," I said.

"He's been working away and won't feel like coming out yet. Maybe we can get together later."

"Okay, Sis, see you later and thanks for breakfast and the roast," I said, hugging her.

"Yeah, a double thanks from me too." Janey gave Josie a hug.

"I'm glad you two have rekindled your friendship. You're good for her, Janey," Josie said. "Keep an eye on her for me?"

"Sure will," Janey said.

Traitor!

I let Josie out.

"I'll call you about line-dancing," I said.

"Okay, bye."

I shut the door and went back to the kitchen where Janey was doing the washing-up. I grabbed the tea towel.

"Gonna keep an eye on me are you?"

"No, of course not. Don't look so worried."

"I'm teasing," I said grinning.

"You bitch." She flicked soapsuds at me.

I flicked the tea towel at her.

"Seriously, can we talk about what happened in Canada?" I asked. "That's if you're not too tired after the flight."

"Not tired at all, yet."

"Okay, let's get this done first, then I'll do some coffee and we can relax in the lounge."

It was a bit chilly so I put the heating on low to take the edge off. I sat in the big armchair and Janey lounged on the sofa.

"So, girlfriend, talk."

"Don't really know where to start, and before you say it, I know I've been guilty of not dealing with this Katie thing."

"True. I could tell that when you saw her again in Canada. I know it was unexpected, but your reaction was exactly what I thought it would be."

"What do you mean?"

"Well, it's so obvious that you're still in love with Katie. It's also obvious that Katie feels something for you."

"Then why doesn't she do anything about it?"

"As I told you before, it's her decision and there's nothing you can do about it."

"So, she's gay and staying in the closet just because of her family and their religious beliefs?"

"Put it this way, she may not be a fully practising Catholic, but she will still have those teachings deep in her from catechism and when she took her first communion," Janey said.

"Yeah, but I know a few Catholic lesbians who just put that to one side and carry on living."

"Yeah, but at what cost to their faith? A lot of people live by their faith, and when that comes into conflict with the way they want to live, something has to give. We all have decisions to make in our lives and some people can't live without their faith."

"But is it Katie's faith or the faith her parents have foisted onto her?"

"We all have faith foisted onto us, don't we? We're sent to the same Sunday school our parents went to. Sometimes we choose a different faith, but often as not we carry on with the one our parents gave us."

What Janey was saying did make some kind of sense. I'd heard of lesbians who were Catholic and didn't live their life to the full. They stayed firmly in the closet. Religion has a lot to answer for. I mean, I look at it from the point of view that God created us and gave us our free will. He gave us a mind of our own. If He didn't want us to use our free will and our own minds, surely He wouldn't have given them to us. As He did give them to us He would expect us to use them, live our lives and be happy. Oh, it's too complicated for me. I just get on with living and try not to complicate things too much. Yes, I know Katie is a complication.

"So, basically, what you're saying is I have to respect her decision and get on with my life," I said, somewhat bitterly.

"That's exactly what I'm saying. It's not going to be easy, but you'll get there. At least with Katie in America you're not likely to bump into her every five minutes."

"I know I've got to move on, but I'm so pissed off. Her decision is the wrong one."

"Wrong for whom, you or her?" Janey asked.

"For the both of us." I took a drink of my coffee.

"You've got to remember that her decision was made taking

everything into consideration. Maybe if she'd decided to come out, her family would have disowned her. She obviously values her family and wouldn't be able to live without them. Could you?"

"No, I guess I couldn't. If I thought I'd have lost Josie, I may have made the same decision as Katie."

"My point exactly. Look, I know this is not what you want to hear right now, but you will get over her. You'll laugh about this in a few months and wonder why you made all this fuss."

"Yeah, you're right. Okay, let's drink to the future," I said, raising my coffee mug. "A future without Katie. It'll be hard to start with, but I know it'll get better," I said, trying to sound positive.

"Yes, it will get better. Trust me, I know these things," Janey said.

"Mmm, you're so like Josie." I said, laughing.

It was so good to have Janey back. It was just a shame we couldn't make it as a couple. Even with Katie off the scene, I knew it still wouldn't work. There wasn't the spark that I felt I had with Katie, even though that was going to go nowhere. Janey yawned. It seemed jet lag was finally catching up on her.

"Come on you, time for bed," I said, dragging Janey to her feet.

"Okay, okay I'm coming," she said, stifling another yawn.

We made our way upstairs.

"You have my room and I'll take the spare," I said.

"Oh, come on, Jess, don't sleep in there. It's cold and you're so warm to sleep with."

"All right, I'll be your personal hot water bottle." I must admit I preferred sleeping on my own, unless I was in a relationship, of course. But it was nice sleeping with Janey. It was comfortable and comforting and I needed that at the moment.

I SLEPT LIKE a log and no, I didn't wake up in the fireplace. When I did finally wake it was nearly midday. I still felt a little tired, but better than I expected. I got up quietly and left Janey to sleep on.

In the kitchen I checked the fridge to see if I needed to pop over to the corner shop. I knew Josie would have stocked up with some basics. She's a great sister and I know I'm lucky to have her. I opened the fridge and saw butter, milk, eggs, bacon, sausages, tomatoes, mushrooms and orange juice. There was fresh bread in the cupboard. Great, we could have a big fry-up. Whenever Janey decided to surface, that is.

I put some coffee in the filter machine and went to the lounge to get my laptop. I sat at the kitchen table with my coffee and checked my emails. Most of it was junk, although I did have a couple telling me how much my life would be improved by getting satellite television. That was something I could do without. I barely had time to watch the five channels I had without adding hundreds more. Oh, and a few insisting I could extend my penis by at least an inch or two. I suppose I could match those with the Viagra emails.

I scanned down the list for personal emails. I only found two, one from Shelley asking how the holiday went and one from Katie. Yes, I know I said I was going to change my email address. Don't you think that would have looked a bit suspicious? Yes. So I decided to leave it as it was. I knew I would have to play it by ear if I ever got one from Katie. I had choices. I could answer it or not as the case may be. So I'd read it, then make a decision,

> Hi Jess
>
> Hope you don't mind me emailing you. I just wanted to say how good it was to see you again. I must admit it was quite a surprise, but a very nice one. What a coincidence eh?
>
> I had a wicked time and meeting Bev and Collette was great. They're a really nice couple. I'm glad you and Janey are together and getting on well. You deserve someone nice, someone who'll be good to you and not mess you about. I really envy you.
>
> Life back in the Big Apple goes on as usual. I'm going for a job interview at long last. It was hard persuading Bill to let me go back to work, but I'm so bored and lonely without my friends. At least if I get a job I'll be able to build up a new circle of friends over here.
>
> Becki and Sidney send their best to you as do I.
> Katie

I read it through a few times and realised she sounded quite low. Maybe life in New York wasn't all she'd hoped. What was that I really envy you line all about? Did she envy me because I was out and happy? Or was it because she and Bill weren't as solid as she thought Janey and I were? Of course I knew Janey and I weren't an item, but Katie didn't. I was surprised that she didn't. Both Bev and Collette knew and I guessed they'd have told Becki and Sidney. Surely one of them would have let it drop, but then why would they?

Now I had to decide whether to reply or not. It was a problem. No, you're right, it's not a problem at all. It's only an email so of course I was going to reply. I tapped away for a few minutes and then read what I'd written:

Hi Katie

Yes, it was nice seeing you too and you're right, what a coincidence! Josie wouldn't believe us at first until I showed her the pictures. (I'm attaching them for you.)

I was glad to see you'd made some friends. Becki and Sidney are very nice. Please send my best back to them. I know they'll look out for you and you'll make more friends when you finally get back to work. Good luck with the interview. It's great you've got Bill to agree to it. You should stand up for yourself more. You're your own person, not an extension of Bill. A relationship is a two way street.

Anyway, enough of the preaching, I'm sure you know what I'm saying.

I don't mind you emailing me this time, but please don't send any more. I think, under the circumstances, it would be better for the both of us.

Jess

Was I being a bit hard telling her how to run her marriage? I suppose maybe a little, but perhaps it was my way of telling her to admit she's gay. Oh, hell, who cares? Yes, I know, I do. Still, she needs to hear it and nobody else is going to tell her.

I pulled up the pictures I'd taken with her in them. I came to the one of us dancing, which told a tale. Should I send it? Yes, why not let her see what she was missing. The devil was in me and I hoped she'd get the same feeling I did when I saw it. Maybe it would make her think. Devious little bugger, aren't I? I attached the lot to the email. I hovered over the send button. Should I or shouldn't I? Finally, I clicked it and the email was sent. That was it, no turning back now. I knew in a way it was a positive move toward getting over Katie. Actually it wasn't really, I was just being bitchy. I wanted her to realise what she'd lost. I sure as hell knew.

I heard a noise behind me and turned round. It was a sleepy-eyed Janey.

"Hi, girlfriend, what you up to?" She asked, groggily. She sat opposite me at the table.

"Just checking my emails. I got one from Katie."

She perked up.

"Oh, did you really?"

"Yeah I did really." I put it on the screen and turned it so Janey could read it.

While she read, I got up and poured two mugs of coffee.

"Not saying much, but saying a lot, if you know what I mean," Janey said, not making much sense at all.

"Okay, I'll buy it, what's she not saying?"

"Well, her comment about us. How glad she is we're together and her envy? She doesn't envy us, she envies me being with you. She wants to be me or at least in my place, well the place she thinks I've got."

"Now I really don't know what you mean."

"It's just that she sounds jealous to me. Why would she mention it at all if she wasn't?"

"How do you know she's jealous? I don't get that at all. Maybe she mentioned it because she genuinely wants me to be happy."

"Yeah, you're probably right. I'm still suffering with jet-lag and reading stuff in to it that's not there."

She started to drink her coffee. "Ah, that's better. Did you reply?"

"I did, do you want to read it?"

I put my reply on the screen for her to read.

"Oh, nice one, that'll make her think and its good you sent it. You need to let her know how you feel so you don't get any more. If she starts emailing you on a regular basis it'll be harder for you," Janey said.

"True. She emails Josie and I don't want her to let on she's emailing me as well. Josie will just put two and two together and make five. I don't want her getting suspicious over nothing. She was bad enough before Katie went to New York."

"Right, we don't want to stir that one up again. Let sleeping dogs lie I say."

"Okay, I'm done here," I said. I shut the laptop down and took it back into the lounge. "Let's get a nice fry-up going. I'm starving."

I went to the fridge and got out all the ingredients for a cholesterol-laden meal. Janey laid the table and organised the fresh coffee while I started grilling bacon, sausages and tomatoes. Yes, I can be healthy as well. No, I'm not going to do scrambled eggs. I have to have a fried egg. It's just not the same with scrambled, is it? No, you see, you know I'm right.

"When we've eaten this," I said between delicious mouthfuls, "we'll go shopping. My cupboards and fridge need replenishing."

Janey grimaced at me. "Great, just what I love, food shopping."

"Don't worry, I hate it too, but we have to eat, so it's in and out before you can say Tesco."

I'd let my food stocks run low before we went away to Canada. Not that I keep much in anyway.

I was true to my word about being quick. From the time we got in to coming out was just over half an hour. Not bad. It was an all-time record for me.

It was getting dark when we got back so we decided to stay in. We were going to have a quiet evening with wine and watch a couple of good DVDs. I'd got two nice juicy steaks for dinner. I don't often do proper meals. There doesn't seem much point for just one. Ah, how sad. After Sue, I'd gone into a decline. But now, since hooking back up with Janey, I was getting the bug to cook again. I do enjoy it, and I'm not bad, though I do say it myself. I suppose the way to do it is to cook for two and put the other portion in the freezer for another day. I decided I'd give it a go. I knew I couldn't keep relying on Josie and eating out.

From my collection of DVDs Janey chose *Notting Hill*. Good choice, I love that film. We started with *Bound*, another favourite.

I positioned the television so I could see it while I pottered about in the kitchen getting dinner ready.

"Don't drag it around like that, let me," Janey said, switching it off and pulling the cables out.

She brought the whole lot into the kitchen. Luckily it's on one of those stands with wheels, so it was quite easy. She plugged it all back in, as we were watching a DVD we didn't need the aerial.

"There," she said, pleased with her handiwork. "We can watch this while you do dinner and we'll eat here too. We can then get comfortable in the lounge for *Notting Hill*."

"Great," I said, looking at her in astonishment.

"It's not rocket science you know," she said. "I do it all the time at home. When I get some spare cash, I'll try and rig mine so I can have a television monitor in the kitchen that runs off the main set."

I grinned, suddenly remembering that Janey's dad, Bernie, was an electrician and really into his gadgets. He'd taught her all she knew, which was quite a lot. I can just about wire a plug. I must get Janey to give me a few lessons.

"Why didn't you go into business with your dad?" I asked her.

"I like to tinker, but didn't fancy it as a career. I much prefer the cut and thrust of big business."

Janey worked in a large advertising agency. She was doing really well for herself with a salary to match. I knew she loved the work and the power dressing, which she carried off with real aplomb. I suppose neither of us could see her dressed in overalls, although she would look very cute. I told her that.

"Not as cute as my low-cut tops under the power trouser suit," she said, laughing.

"Well, I'll have to remember how good you are with this electrical stuff. Next time I get a problem, I'll be on the phone for help."

"No probs, my call out is—"

She ducked as I threw the dishcloth at her.

Janey put the DVD in and pressed play.

We prepared dinner together, just like an old married couple. Coming to this conclusion at the same time we looked at each other and grinned.

After we'd eaten and watched the film, Janey took the television back to the lounge and connected it back up. I did the washing up, and then took a fresh bottle of wine and the glasses into the lounge for the second film. Janey was stretched out on the sofa. I poured us both a glass of wine and flopped in the armchair. Once we were settled, Janey pressed play and we watched *Notting Hill*. By the time it had finished I was in tears. Yes, I know, soppy cow.

"What's up?" Janey asked as she sat up.

"Why can't love be that easy?" I asked, pointing to the movie as the credits rolled up.

"Well, it wasn't to start with, was it? I mean old Hugh and Julia didn't have a smooth relationship until the end," Janey replied.

"I suppose so. It's not gonna happen like that for me and Katie, is it?"

"No, it's not. You need to accept that."

"Yeah, I know. It's just that they looked so happy and content at the end."

"It's not real life."

I glared at Janey. "I know that, but it does happen, doesn't it? I mean it must have a basis in fact to make it believable."

"Okay, okay, sorry you're right, but don't go thinking that's gonna happen to you and Katie, girlfriend."

"I know what you're saying. I'm sorry I snapped. You're right. I know it's not gonna happen to me and Katie, and I know I need to accept that fact."

"That's enough sadness. Let's have something lighter," Janey said, getting up to choose something.

Chapter Eleven

I SLEPT BADLY and woke feeling more tired than when I went to bed. I stumbled into the kitchen to make some coffee. Janey was sitting at the table eating toast and reading a book.

"Hi, girlfriend. God, you look wrecked."

"Oh that's charming. You certainly know how to knock a girl down. I didn't sleep at all well," I said, indignantly. "Any coffee left?"

"Yeah, a little, I'll make some more." She poured me a mug and put more water into the filter machine with fresh grounds.

"I think we should go to Brighton today," Janey said, cheerily. "It'll wake you up."

"Okay," I said, less than enthusiastically.

"You'll enjoy it when we get there, trust me. I'll drive and you can kip on the way down."

"It's a plan," I said, brightening up. I really didn't fancy driving.

I did sleep all the way, only waking as Janey parked the car.

"Well, girlfriend, you obviously needed that sleep," she said, grinning at me.

"Yeah, I feel much better now." I got out of the car and stretched. It was great being by the sea and I loved it.

"Okay, a nice brisk walk to town, have some lunch, then we'll hit the shops," Janey said, linking her arm through mine.

"Not too brisk. I need to work up to it," I said, slowing her down.

Although it was May it was still a little chilly, but at least it was sunny, hardly a cloud in the sky and the wind was quite gentle. I'd brought my camera along and stopped every now and again, to take pictures of the sun on the sea.

"I really love being by the sea in the spring," I said, as we walked.

"Me too, it's lovely and fresh. It blows away all the cobwebs," Janey said.

By the time we got to the town I was starving. We found a nice café and ordered cheese toasties and coffee as we were saving ourselves for dinner later.

"So, where we gonna shop?" I asked. I already knew what Janey's answer would be.

"The Lanes, of course."

I knew she loved looking in all the little shops. They sell such lovely stuff and as I've said before, I too enjoy shopping in the Lanes. Trouble is, I could spend a fortune so it's a good job I don't have one then.

"That sounds good to me and after that can we go on the pier? I fancy blowing a load on the fruit machines."

"Got the gambling bug?"

"Oh yeah, I'll spend at least a fiver."

I loved going in the arcade on the pier with all those machines clattering away and people playing them with such intensity. Me, I just set myself a limit and stick to it. Yes, I know, boring, but at least I knew I wouldn't go bankrupt. I was sensible as I knew you could never win much. If you could the pier would be out of business in no time.

We finished our lunch and headed for the Lanes. It was quite busy with sightseers even this early in the season.

One of the shops we went into had lots of mobiles hanging from the ceiling and no, not those kind of mobiles. I found one I really liked. It was shells on a single thick strand of string with a blue wooden dolphin in the middle of it. It was really nice and I could picture it hanging in my bathroom.

"I'm gonna get that one," I said, to Janey, pointing at it.

"Go for it, girlfriend. I take it you're gonna put it in the bathroom?"

"Nah, I thought I'd hang it in the kitchen."

We bumped hips and grinned at each other.

"I'm gonna get that one." She pointed to one on three strands of thin cord and connected by a brightly coloured wooden ring. The three strands had painted wooden fish of varying bright colours spaced down them. It was really nice and would look good in her bathroom.

"Take it yours is for the lounge then?"

I ducked away to the cash register to pay for my purchase.

We carried on wandering round the Lanes, checking out the shops. I bought some nice smelling bath oils and scented candles.

"Very nice," Janey said, as we took them to the till.

"Yeah, I'll save them for when I'm not bathing alone."

"Well, let's hope that won't be before they've passed their sell by date," she said.

"Oh yes, very funny."

By the time we got to the pier it was getting dark. The bright lights stood out against the blackness of the sea and sky beyond. It looked quite lovely so I took a couple of pictures using the night mode, hoping they would come out all right.

It didn't take me long to get rid of my fiver, but I had fun doing it. Janey had more luck and came out a fiver up, which was probably mine.

"You know what they say?"

"What?" Janey asked.

"Lucky at cards, unlucky at love," I said, laughing.

"So, you're gonna get lucky, are you?"

"Yeah, maybe I am."

"Well, you go for it, girlfriend."

"Drinks are on you then are they, as you won?"

"It was only—yeah sure, I know you need cheering up after losing such a large amount."

"I'll ignore that remark," I said, as we made our way back to the car. "Do you want me to drive back?"

"Thanks, I could do with a drink after all that retail therapy." She handed me the keys.

I DROVE TO the Harvester on the outskirts of the town. We're definitely the last of the big spenders. We were shown to a table and our drinks order taken. Our waitress left us with the menus to decide what we wanted.

A few minutes later Janey's lager and my orange juice arrived. We ordered our food, Janey decided on the plantation platter and I pushed out the boat with a fillet steak. Blow the expense. Actually it wasn't that bad, but after the holiday I wasn't very flush. Still, only a week to pay day, I could survive.

"Twelve o'clock," Janey whispered.

I looked up, but couldn't see anyone. Then I realised twelve o'clock was behind me.

"What?"

"A really good looking woman has just come in," she said, still in a whisper.

Suddenly she smiled, but not at me. The waitress seated the mystery woman a table to the side of us, but I still couldn't see her clearly.

"She smiled at me," Janey said. She was like a nervous teenager.

"Maybe she was just being friendly. You were staring at her when she came in."

"She probably thought I was looking at you," Janey said.

"No, I doubt it. There's no mistaking the drool on your chin." I laughed at her. I'd not seen Janey like this before.

I turned to have a quick glance at the object of Janey's stare.

I managed to take in a very attractive woman. I guessed her to be in her late twenties or early thirties. She had long blonde hair and a nice smile. Oops, she caught me, so much for being discreet. I turned back quickly.

"She looks nice," I said to Janey. "She's got a nice smile too."

"Yeah, I noticed that," Janey said. "Look, bear with me a few minutes. I've got to go over."

She got up before I could stop her.

I sat drinking my orange juice, waiting for our food to come and Janey to return. Both happened simultaneously.

"I got her phone number," Janey said, waving a piece of paper in front of me. "Her name's Lucy and she's a solicitor."

"Okay, does she live in Brighton? Is she single and is she sane?"

"No, yes and I think so," Janey said, and we both laughed.

"I don't know why I worry about that, none of us are," I said.

"What? Living in Brighton, single and sane?"

"No, sane," I said, with a laugh.

"Another woman's sat down with her," said Janey. "And she kissed her."

"Don't worry. I'm sure she wouldn't lie that blatantly with you sitting a few feet away."

"Only kidding. She told me it's her mum's birthday and she's treating her to dinner."

"So, you gonna give her a ring then?"

"Is the Pope a Catholic?"

"Point taken, if it were me I'd certainly give her a ring. She looks like a nice person. She's got an open friendly face."

"What does that mean, an open face?" Janey popped a forkful of food in her mouth.

"I guess for me it means someone not trying to hide anything, someone genuine. I know what I mean, but I'm not doing so well at explaining," I said, getting more than a little confused. I chewed on my steak and thought.

"It's okay, I understand what you're trying and failing to explain," Janey said, grinning. "I just wanted to see if you knew what you meant."

"You've got the devil in you now and I can guess why. You're really attracted to Lucy, aren't you?"

I could read Janey like a book sometimes. I knew how she was around women she was attracted to. She became hyper and could easily make a prat of herself.

"Yeah, she's really good looking, but that's not it. She seems like a nice person. I felt really comfortable going over to her. It was as if she wanted me to. I think we really clicked."

We continued eating as we talked.

"I'm pleased for you. It's time you found someone to settle

down with."

"Well, don't get me married off yet, I've only just met her," Janey said, with a grin.

"Yeah, you're right. Just give her a call and take it from there."

We finished our meal and sat chatting over a final drink before making a move. As we got up to leave Lucy came over.

"Don't forget to call me," she said, and gave Janey a kiss on the cheek.

"I won't, don't worry."

We made our way out to the car. Once inside I screamed and hit the steering wheel.

"Boy, has she got it bad," I said.

"Well, what can you expect? I'm quite a catch."

"Okay, okay, I won't need to drive you home. You'll be able to float."

"I must admit I was surprised she came over to remind me to ring. Maybe she's desperate."

"Maybe she is. Maybe she'll stalk you if you don't call her."

Janey looked at me to see if I was serious. I couldn't keep a straight face and burst out laughing.

"That's not funny." Janey thumped me.

"Ouch! I guess I deserved that," I said, rubbing my arm.

"Yeah, don't rain on my parade."

"Have you thought that maybe she just wanted to kiss you?" I asked. "She's really got to you, hasn't she?"

"No, of course not," Janey said, a little too casually.

"So, when are you gonna ring her?"

We'd travelled in silence for about ten minutes. I guessed Janey was still a bit pissed off at me for earlier.

"I'll wait 'til I get back to mine."

"You gonna make her wait then?"

Janey was quiet and looking straight ahead.

"You've not lost your bottle, have you?"

"No, I guess I'm just nervous," she replied.

"She has got to you." I kept my voice neutral. I didn't want Janey to think I was teasing her again.

"Yeah, she has. Something happened between us while we were in the restaurant. I can't explain it."

I could. The same thing had happened to me, in another lifetime, it seemed.

"Well, she seems very nice. Give her a call. You'll never know what could happen if you don't try."

"Don't worry, I'm gonna give her a ring. I just need to do it in private."

"That's fine, but don't forget to let me know how it goes. I want all the details."

"Girlfriend, I'll record it for you if you want."

Janey sounded more like her usual positive self and by the time we got home we were in good spirits.

The holiday was over and Janey was going back home tomorrow. I was sad that she was leaving. I liked having her around. Maybe I should think about getting a lodger? Nah. I like my independence too much. It would be all right if Janey were looking to share, but with a possible new relationship on the horizon, I knew she'd want her own space. Besides, why would she sell her place to come and share mine? Not good sense at all. It wasn't as if I needed the money, but the company would be nice. Still, I'd soon get used to being alone again. Working shifts was quite good for that. It just wasn't good for fitting in a life, but I managed.

We spent what was left of the night chatting and finishing off a bottle of wine while Janey finished off her packing. That night we slept curled up together in friendly companionship.

"I'm gonna miss you, Janey," I said, as she brought her bags down the next morning.

"Me too, girlfriend." She gave me a big hug. "But you don't get rid of me that easily. I'm gonna keep in touch this time, so you'll see a lot more of me."

"We'll see. When you ring Lucy you'll be too involved with her. You'll forget all about me." I tried to pout and look sad.

"No, I won't. I promise," Janey said, not picking up on my teasing.

"For God's sake, Janey, I'm joking. The three of us can all go out together, so I know I'll see you, you idiot."

"Sorry, I guess I'm being over sensitive, aren't I?"

"You sure are. Listen, go home, call Lucy and let me know what happens."

"Yeah, I'll call you later. Thanks for a great time, girlfriend. I've really enjoyed it."

I helped her out to the car.

"Right, don't forget to call Lucy." I gave her a big hug.

"As if," Janey said. "Call you later."

"You'd better. Drive safely."

I watched her down the road and then slowly walked back inside to my lonely quiet little house. Oh dear, how sad. Never mind.

"RIGHT EVERYONE, NOW please. I've got a few words to say," I said, getting everyone's attention.

The gang was all here, Josie, Shelley, Lou, Lisa, Mel and Lori. Plus Janey and Lucy, who were now firmly part of the gang.

They'd really hit it off from their first date and were well loved-up. It was great to see Janey so happy. They were so committed to each other that they were talking about buying a house together next spring.

"So here we are, the inaugural barbecue on my new patio, no spilling drinks. Seriously, I can't believe it's the middle of August already. It seems only last week Janey and I came back from Canada, full of the joys of spring. Well, Janey was anyway."

I looked at Janey and Lucy sitting close and looking good together.

"I'm so glad Lucy found her and is gonna make an honest woman of her—no mean task that. Anyway, to all of you, welcome and have fun today. The neighbours have been warned there's a bunch of loony lezzies loose, but please don't run amok in the garden." I finished and held up my glass. "Let's drink to a good summer." Everyone cheered and joined in the toast.

"Jess, that was a nice speech," Josie said, giving me a kiss on the cheek. "Mum and Dad would be pleased with what you've done."

"Yeah, I guess they would. I knew they had plans to put a patio in. I just put those plans into motion. And no, I didn't do it because they wanted it, but because I did and it's a great space for parties."

"I know, Jess. You've worked hard and saved hard to make the house yours and you've stamped your own style and personality on it which is good. I'd be worried if you'd turned it into a shrine," Josie said, gently.

"God, no, I'd never do that. I loved Mum and Dad, but I know they'd turn in their graves if I didn't do what I wanted with the house. It was their legacy for us to create our own space. I love that I'm living in their house, but knowing it's mine. If you know what I mean."

"Yeah, I do and I'm proud of you. I just wish you could find someone to share it with."

"One day I'm sure I will, now let's party."

I'd done a buffet in the kitchen and put bottles of beer and wine in my old bath filled with ice. I must get rid of it or make it into a proper feature. It'd been in the garden for ages, ever since I'd redone the bathroom.

Lisa and Shelley were cooking at the barbecue and looked like they were enjoying themselves.

"Hi, guys, having fun?"

"Yeah, you?" Lisa answered.

"Great ta." I helped myself to a chicken leg, sausage and burger.

"Janey and Lucy look well loved-up," Shelley said.

We all looked over.

"Yeah, she deserves some happiness," I said.

"Yeah, so do you. When are you gonna settle down?" Lisa asked.

"When you do," I replied, and headed for the kitchen.

I loaded up my plate with salad and other bits. I was just about to return to the garden when the doorbell rang. I hoped it wasn't a neighbour complaining, not that they could really, as the music wasn't very loud, nor was the gang. Still, it was only about four, it would probably get noisier later on.

I opened the door and my jaw hit the floor. It was Katie. A pregnant Katie!

"Hi, hope you don't mind. Josie said it would be all right. I've come straight from the airport and I've already let the cab go. Josie wanted to pick me up, but I told her not to worry." She smiled that smile and my legs went to jelly.

"Er, yeah, er, you'd better come in." I held the door open for her. "We're all in the garden," I said as I closed the door. "Go straight out and I'll follow. Do you want a drink?" I tried to sound casual now I'd recovered some composure.

"Yeah, orange juice please. You look good, Jess," she said and looked deep into my eyes.

Shit! That's the composure gone again. She could do it every time and I thought I was getting over her. Oh yes, of course I was.

"Oh, thanks. You er look—" I was lost for words.

"Pregnant. Yeah, I know. Josie should have warned you I was coming," she said, sadly.

"She probably wanted it to be a surprise."

And it was certainly that. Still, I guess I had the answer to my question. Katie had decided, emphatically, on the straight life. At least now I knew once and for all.

"Look, let me get your drink. Actually you'd better follow me out. I can't let you into the garden without an announcement. You'll get mobbed."

"Thank you, Jess, you're always so thoughtful."

I got Katie her drink and led the way to the garden.

"Hey, everyone, look who's just turned up," I shouted.

I stepped aside to let Katie through.

Well, all hell broke loose. Now I was worried about the neighbours.

Everyone crowded round Katie and started asking questions all at once. I grabbed a chair and forced a way to her.

"Quiet everyone. Let Katie sit and catch her breath," I said, getting her to sit.

I stepped back and watched Katie from the kitchen door. My mind was in turmoil and I saw Josie looking up at me. How long had she been watching me looking at Katie? I quickly smiled and raised my glass. She smiled back. I went into the kitchen to make sure the buffet wasn't dried up and to replenish the salad. I was busy sorting it out and didn't hear Janey come in.

"You okay, girlfriend?"

"Yeah, course. You want some more food? I must get some more bread. And we'll need more fresh salad done. It's nearly all gone. You lot are eating as if you'd never eaten before." I busied myself with cutting up the bread.

"Stop it!" Janey grabbed the knife and put it on the side.

She turned me to face her. The tears were starting to flow down my cheeks. She pulled me to her and gave me a hug and I held on to her letting the tears flow.

"It's okay, girlfriend, just let it all out," she said, gently rubbing my back.

"Jess! What's up?" It was Josie.

"It's the emotion of the day. You know, what we were talking about earlier. I'll be all right in a bit. Just let me go and splash some water on my face."

I left Janey and Josie and went up to the bathroom.

Shit! Shit! Shit! That was close. I didn't want Josie asking awkward questions. Why did Katie have to turn up now? Why did Josie tell her to come over without letting me know? Oh well, it was done now. I splashed my face several times with cold water and dried it off. Mmm, I wasn't looking too bad and my eyes weren't that red. If I went straight back down to the kitchen and cut up an onion for the salad, I could get away with it. God, I can be so devious it scares me.

I went back down and fortunately the kitchen was empty. I grabbed an onion and started peeling it. The tears were in full flow when Josie returned.

"Are you sure you're all right?" she asked, and I could hear the concern in her voice.

"Yeah, it's the onion now," I said.

"Okay, is there anymore orange juice? Katie needs a refill."

I went to the fridge and got a fresh carton out.

"I'll just finish refreshing this tired old salad and be right out," I said.

"Okay," Josie said, and took the carton of orange out to the patio.

I watched the gang from the kitchen window. They were all crowded round Katie, getting the latest on what had been happening to her.

I took my time over the salad. Not because I really cared about it, I just needed time to compose myself. Finally I had to go out. I couldn't hide in the kitchen any longer.

"Katie's been telling us what's been happening to her in New York," Mel said.

"I would have thought that was obvious," I said.

I didn't actually mean it to come out the way it did. I just hoped no one caught the edge in my voice. There was silence for what seemed like ages. Then everyone fell about laughing. They thought I'd made a joke.

"Oh, very funny, Jess," Shelley said.

"I aim to please," I said, grinning. "Come on, everyone, there's still a stack of food to get through."

The rest of the afternoon and evening went well. Everyone seemed to be enjoying themselves. I avoided talking for any length to Katie, spending most of the time getting food and drink and keeping the music going.

"I'm gonna take Katie home. She's still jet-lagged and needs to get some sleep," Josie said. It was nearly ten o'clock.

"Yeah, I'm sure she is," I said.

"Are you all right?"

"Yeah, parties are hard work when you throw them. I'm just a bit tired too."

"Okay, we'll see ourselves out. I'll call you tomorrow to see if you need a hand clearing up."

"Don't worry about it, Josie. Janey and Lucy are staying over and I'm off tomorrow so it's no bother."

"Okay, if you're sure."

Josie went back into the garden and I watched her and Katie say their goodbyes. They came into the kitchen and I walked them to the front door.

"Bye, Jess, great party. Thanks, it was good to see you again," Katie said.

"You're welcome. It was good to see you again too," I said, calmly.

I closed the door behind them and stood leaning against it. I couldn't move, I felt numb. I just wanted everyone to leave, but it was still early. I managed to pull myself together and went back into the kitchen. I looked at all my friends enjoying themselves and I knew I couldn't spoil their evening by behaving like a wet blanket, so I grabbed a beer and went and joined them. I actually ended up having a good time and I even got a little pissed, which helped loosen me up.

FINALLY, JUST AFTER two in the morning, the last of them left. As Janey and Lucy were staying the night, we did clear up a bit and then sat at the kitchen table with a nightcap.

"So, girlfriend, how you doing?" Janey asked.

"Not too bad, I think."

"Come on, Jess. I haven't known you that long, but even I can tell you're not doing that well," Lucy said, looking at Janey, who nodded in agreement.

She was such a nice person. They made a really good couple and were so in love. Lucy was very intuitive and she was also right, I wasn't doing very well at all.

"No, I'm not okay. I was 'til Katie arrived. I thought I'd gone a long way to getting over her. How wrong can I be?"

"Well, what are you gonna do? You can't hide away forever."

"I really don't know, Janey. What do you mean, hide away forever?"

"Katie's back for quite a while."

"Define, quite a while?" I had this sinking feeling in the pit of my stomach.

"Er..."

"Janey! Come on, how long?"

"Definitely until after the birth at the end of December, but I get the impression it may be longer," Lucy said gently.

Janey had told Lucy all about me and Katie. Not that there's much to tell really, but then if there wasn't much to tell I wouldn't feel like this. The minute Katie and I kissed all those months ago everything changed, for me at least, but obviously not for the now pregnant Katie.

"Why, what did she say?"

The thought of Katie being around again and not be able to be with her was awful.

"It's not what she said. It's what she didn't say that spoke volumes," Lucy said.

"So you don't know for sure?"

"No, I don't."

"Jess, relax. Everything will be okay," Janey said.

"Yeah, you're right. Let's face it, nothing's changed. She's still straight and that's now quite obvious." I caught a look between Janey and Lucy. "What?"

"Lucy thinks the same as me, that Katie's gay."

"That's as may be, but it's not the point, is it? She's made her decision."

"That's right and you have to get on with your life," Lucy said, trying to get me to be positive.

"Easier said than done." I looked at them both. "But I'll try.

Honestly I will."

"Good, the first step is to get you out more. You've hardly been out since Canada," Janey said.

"I know, I just haven't felt like it, but I promise to get my act together."

"Let's make a date to go to Nexus next weekend then, if you're off," Lucy said.

"Yes I am. All weekend, so I can make it. Shall we get the rest of the gang to come as well?"

"That's a good idea. Let's go and have a real good night out," Janey said.

I must admit, for the first time in ages, I was looking forward to going out. I just needed someone to push me. The others had tried, but I was clever and just kept telling them I was working. I couldn't use that excuse all the time, 'cos I didn't work all the time and they knew that. Then I just had to bite the bullet and go out. I usually enjoyed myself, but I really wasn't up for it to start with. It's always the way, isn't it? You don't want to go out, and then you go and have a great time. I just have trouble galvanising myself into action. I've even turned down a couple of one-night stands. God, I must be in love. Well, that was true, and anyway how do you go about falling out of love? I never had any problem before. Ah, but then I guess I wasn't really in love before.

Maybe Big G should have given us a switch in our brains. That way we could switch love off whenever we wanted. But I guess that'd be too convenient for some people.

"Right, that's settled then. We'll have a great time," Lucy said.

"Yeah, we'll find you a nice woman," Janey said, grinning salaciously.

"I don't think I'm ready for that yet."

"At this rate you'll never be ready," Janey said.

"Look, I've said I'll go out. Can we leave it at that?"

"Yes, Janey. Let Jess work through it at her own pace and in her own way," Lucy said.

"Okay, I promise not to set you up. Although the woman I had in mind is really cute."

Lucy gave Janey a look.

"Well, she is, but not as cute as you," Janey said, grinning.

Chapter Twelve

SATURDAY MORNING ARRIVED and I felt a sense of dread at what the evening would be like. I didn't know whether I could trust Janey not to set something up, even with Lucy keeping an eye on her. I'd been out so seldom since February that I really couldn't be bothered any more, which is really sad. I knew I needed to start going out again or end up a recluse with matted hair and long fingernails. Have you ever got to the stage where you just can't get yourself going? It becomes such a habit, not going out, that it's like trying to walk through treacle and you can't be bothered anymore. It becomes so hard to change back. I'd just have to pull myself together.

It was obvious Katie had made her decision to stay with Bill and have the baby. But why was she back in England for the birth? I thought the hospitals in America were good. Mind you, if ER is anything to go by, I can understand her coming back. There were times that a simple pregnancy could end in death during that series. Yes, I do know it's only fiction. Maybe it was the cost of health insurance, which I know is very high in America. But then surely Bill could afford it. Maybe Katie just wanted to be home, so she could have her family around her. I didn't know. I just knew it had set me back from getting over her.

I made myself some breakfast and strong coffee. I needed to fortify myself for tonight. Maybe I could feign a sudden serious illness like an inoperable tumour? Yes, I know it's a tad drastic, but hey, that's how I was feeling. Maybe I could put on a cold over the phone. It would be quite easy. No, I had to go out and get back into the swing of things.

After breakfast I showered, put on a pair of shorts and a vest top and went out into the garden. It was a lovely sunny day and a shame to waste it indoors, especially now I had my new patio. It was only midday so I resisted the temptation of alcohol. I can be sensible sometimes. Besides, I'd probably have plenty tonight. I'd need to anaesthetise myself to get through the evening. I made a long drink of ice, fresh orange and lemonade, and grabbed a book. Looking at the title, *Hunter's Way*, I put it back and chose a James Patterson instead. I could do without a story about a gay woman and a straight woman right now. I sat on one of the comfy sun loungers and put the parasol up to give me some shade. Only mad dogs and Englishmen go out in the midday sun. As I was neither of those I put the lounger right out in the sun. After about half an hour I was having trouble reading. The strong sunlight was reflecting on the white pages. It was really hot, so I pulled the parasol closer and relaxed.

There was a persistent ringing in my ears and I woke up with a start. I'd obviously dozed off in the heat. God, I'm getting to be like an old woman having an afternoon nap. The ringing stopped and then started again. As I slowly came too, I realised it was my doorbell. I can be quite bright sometimes you know. I got up and went to answer it. I checked the clock in the kitchen, three thirty, which meant I'd been asleep for a couple of hours. I must remember to get some Sanatogen.

I opened the door to find Katie standing there looking very hot and bothered.

"Okay, okay, enough with the ringing," I said, testily.

"Sorry. I'm just really hot. I was sure you were in. Josie said you'd be in."

"As you can see, I am in. You'd better come in and sit down before you pass out," I said, ushering her in.

While she settled herself at the kitchen table, I got both of us cold drinks.

"I'm sorry if I've disturbed you, just coming round like this," Katie said.

She took a long drink.

"Yeah, you have disturbed me."

Katie looked at me and I saw she was on the verge of tears. My words were a bit harsh, I know.

"Sorry, I didn't mean to snap. I'd fallen asleep in the garden and you ringing the doorbell startled me awake."

"I know what that's like. It takes ages to wake up properly."

"And you feel like shit for hours. Well I do anyway."

"Me too," Katie said, drinking some more.

"So, to what do I owe the pleasure?" I asked, trying to shake off the just woke-up feeling.

"Josie said you'd probably be in. She and Ivan have gone off to do some shopping and they dropped me off on the way. I've got some stuff from Becki and Sidney for you."

"I usually chill at home if I've got the weekend off. I get so few that I make the most of them. Then out in the evening for a wild night," I said, trying to sound as if I went out all the time and really enjoyed it.

Katie delved into her bag and brought out a couple of neatly wrapped packages.

"Becki and Sidney send their love. They want to know when you and Janey are going to visit, although I suppose Lucy will come as well," Katie said, looking straight at me.

I realised she was referring to Janey and I pretending to be together. But what did it matter to her anyway?

"Just because Janey and I shared a room and a bed, didn't mean we were an item. It saved on a room, especially as Bev and Collette were expecting people for the weekend."

"I know, I just put two and two together."

"And you made five."

Katie laughed. "All right, don't make fun of me."

The way we were talking was as if we'd never been apart. She was a great friend. Pity she couldn't be a lover as well.

"I'm not. I've missed you," I said. "Talking with you is so easy."

It slipped out before I could stop it.

Katie reached out and covered my hand. It was like an electric shock travelling right through me, reaching right down to my core.

"I've missed you too," she said, looking deep into my eyes.

I moved my hand and got up. I switched the kettle on and started to make coffee. I needed something to do. With my back turned to Katie I tried to get my feelings in check. It was hard because she looked so sexy. Being pregnant suited her.

I turned back to the table from getting the coffee cups to realise Katie was right behind me. I nearly dropped the cups. She put them on the table and took my face in her hands and kissed me. I just couldn't help myself, I kissed her back. Oh, come on, in the same situation you'd have done the same. I remember those kisses so well, they were forever etched in my memory and I was lost again in the moment and was really enjoying it. She moved her hands down to my breasts. Oh my God! I was only wearing a vest top and no bra. The thrill was instantaneous. My nipples were erect and my breathing erratic. I put my hands on her buttocks, pulled her pelvis into mine and started to move against her. Katie moved her hands to the bottom of my vest top and pulled it up to reveal my rock-hard nipples. She stopped kissing me and started kissing my left breast. Trust her to pick the most sensitive one. Isn't it funny how one can get you going more than the other? I started to unbutton her blouse, revealing a lacy bra holding her beautiful breasts. I reached round and undid it. I'm really good at that, one hand and it's undone. I lifted her head so I could kiss her again. I was so thoroughly aroused by now I could feel the wetness and wanted to feel Katie's fingers inside me. Katie pulled away after a long kiss and looked at me. There was no mistaking that look and I looked back at her. Her face, her breasts then down to her stomach. I saw the bulge of her pregnancy and froze. That was definitely a passion killer. How did I not feel the bump when I pulled Katie to me? Well, in the throes of passion I forgot everything.

I pulled my top down, pulled Katie's blouse together and moved away from her.

"What's up?" she asked.

"What the hell do you think you're doing? More to the point, what the hell am I doing?" I'd let her do it to me again. No, I'd let myself get carried away so I really couldn't blame it all on Katie.

"I would've thought that was obvious," she replied, matching my tone of voice.

I was angry, but I was angrier with myself for letting it happen. How far was Katie going to go to have sex with a woman? Couldn't she have got it out of her system in New York? I'm sure there were plenty of dykes who would have obliged. Hell, once upon a time I would have. Not anymore, not with Katie. I cared too much about my sanity to go down that road. Not that I had much sanity left, but what I did have I wanted to preserve. What on earth would Josie say if she knew why Katie came round here? She'd kill me. Well, maybe not kill, but she'd be very disappointed in me and I couldn't bear that.

"You want something from me I'm not prepared to give," I said, "and you're pregnant with Bill's baby for God's sake."

"Don't you think I know that?"

I guess it was an obvious statement to make.

"Things aren't going well between us," she said sadly.

"Oh, so you thought you'd come back and try it on with me? You made your choice."

"Maybe it was the wrong one," she said, in a quiet voice.

Now she tells me. But what difference would it make? Would she change her mind the minute Bill snapped his fingers?

"Wrong or right, it was your choice and I'm not getting involved. It's too complicated."

It was complicated and I didn't want to get involved. If she had come back and told me she was getting a divorce. If she had realised she was gay. If she had said she wanted to make a go of it with me. If she had not been pregnant—then, maybe, just maybe, things would have been different. But to come back to try and seduce me with no explanation, well, that was just too much. I suppose now I could see it from the other side. Before Josie's challenge, I was a love 'em and leave 'em lover. I must have hurt so many women and now I could see why. It wasn't right and I wasn't proud of myself at that moment. But at least I was now trying to make amends by being more true to myself about what I wanted. Yes, I wanted Katie more than I could say, but the cost was too high. The regrets would come and it would be ruined. It wouldn't last because it would have been built on lies and deceit.

"I think you'd better go. We have nothing further to say to each other."

I walked to the front door.

"Jess, please don't leave it like this."

"Katie, go back to Josie's, please. We'll forget this ever happened, put it behind us."

"There's something between us. You know it and I know it. Sooner or later you're going to have to admit it!"

She was right about that, but I wasn't about to tell her.

"How dare you! This is the second time you've led me up the garden path and the second time you've made me feel a fool. But it's the last time. Just get out and leave me alone. I never want to see you again."

I yanked the door open and watched her go.

I slammed the door shut behind her. Then the guilt hit me. How was she going to get back to Josie's? It was really hot and she was upset. There was a cab office just down the road, I'm sure she could manage. I stood looking at the closed door. Should I go after her and make sure she got a cab? Should I get the car and drive her home?

I opened the door and Katie was about to ring the bell.

"I'll drive you back to Josie's," I said, grabbing my keys from the hook. I shut the front door and got in the car.

We drove in silence to Josie's and I let Katie out. I didn't wait around. I just drove straight back home. At least now I didn't feel so bad about chucking her out.

I GOT BACK from Josie's feeling like shit. But at least I'd not let Katie make her own way there. I'd never have forgiven myself if anything had happened to her.

I looked at the clock in the kitchen and saw there were only a couple of hours before I was meeting the gang to go out. Flying to the moon would have been easier than getting up the enthusiasm to go out to Nexus. Janey would really be on my case if I cried off now. What I needed was something to eat and drink and then I'd feel a lot better. It was ages since breakfast. What with falling asleep and Katie turning up, I realised hunger was causing my bad mood.

I made myself chicken in white wine sauce and rice. No, I didn't make the sauce. That came courtesy of a jar. Once I'd eaten I began to feel much better. I had a glass of wine with my meal and another while I lazed in the bath. Very decadent I know, but nice and relaxing.

I dressed in black jeans and a white vest top. It was still hot, so

I didn't bother with a shirt or jacket. I checked myself in the full-length mirror and was pleased with what I saw. Now I was in the mood to go out and have some fun. It'd been too long. Women beware.

"HI, GUYS," I said, as I joined the gang in the pub. "Anyone want a drink?"

"No ta," Mel said, "I've just got a round in. Let me get yours while you sit down."

"Thanks. I'll have a pint, please."

"Yeah, sit down, Jess. It must have been a shock to your system to actually come out," Lou said.

"Oh ha, ha, you're so funny."

"Well, it has been a while since you've been out with us," Lori said.

"We were beginning to think you'd got a secret woman stashed away," Shelley said.

"Who, me? I wish."

If only they knew what had been going on.

"Yeah, you," Shelley said. "You've been very quiet lately."

"I've been working hard and when I did have time off I was too tired." I knew I was lying, but could hardly tell them the real reason.

"No more excuses, you're gonna come out more even if we have to drag you," Mel said, as she put my pint on the table.

"Okay, I promise not to be a bore. Anyway, where are Janey and Lucy? This was all their idea and they're not here yet."

"They went round to Josie's to get Katie to come out," Shelley said.

My heart sank. The last thing I wanted was to see Katie tonight. Just then Janey and Lucy came in, followed by Josie and no Katie. Thank God.

"Hi, guys. We managed to drag Josie out, but Katie's not feeling too good," Janey said.

I felt a little guilty, as it was probably because of our run in that afternoon that Katie had decided to stay in.

"I'll get some drinks," Lucy said, as Josie and Janey joined us at the table.

We had a couple of drinks at the pub before moving on to Nexus.

I decided I was going to have a good time. I got a chaser with my next pint to get me in the mood.

I looked round and saw a couple of nice-looking women who might be interesting to get to know. Well, I've got to get over Katie somehow. Don't worry, I'm not going to go back to my old ways.

"Right, I'm off to the dance floor. If I don't come back in half an hour, don't send a search party," I said as I left the rest of them chatting.

They would, no doubt, join me later. I walked over to one of the women I'd noticed to see if she fancied a dance. She didn't, nor did the other three or four I asked. Boy, was I losing my touch. Either that or maybe they sensed my heart really wasn't in it. I decided to go back to the gang.

"That was quick. Have you lost your magic touch?" Josie asked.

"No, there wasn't anyone I fancied," I said.

"Yeah, right. I saw you asking those women and I saw them turn you down," Josie said, grinning. "You've lost your mojo."

"No, I reckon she has got a woman stashed away," Shelley said.

Was I imagining it or did Josie give me a look?

"I've already told you there's no-one, honestly," I said, trying not to get angry. I was worried about Josie and her intuition clicking in. She had an uncanny knack of sussing me out.

"Who wants a drink, then? It must be my round," I said, diverting the attention off me and my non-existent love life.

I got the orders and went to the bar. Janey came with me to help.

"You need to watch it. I think Josie's becoming suspicious," Janey said, as we waited for our drinks.

"Katie came round this afternoon and virtually threw herself at me."

"Jesus, Jess, this is getting out of hand."

"I know, tell me about it. I'll just have to make sure I keep out of her way from now on."

"That's not exactly gonna be easy is it, with her staying at Josie's?"

"I'll work it out. Don't worry." I picked up the drinks and took them back to the table.

"Right, you lot, let's get this evening on the go. Who wants a tequila slammer?" I was determined to blot Katie out tonight. If getting totally wrecked was the only way, then so be it.

THE JACKHAMMER WAS really loud and woke me up. My eyes took a while to focus and I couldn't work out where I was. Then I realised the jack hammer was in my head. I knew this because it never stopped. Even the most hard-working labourer would have to stop every now and again, to lift up the bit of road or whatever they needed to lift up. I closed my eyes again, but the jackhammer was not going to let up. I re-opened my eyes and tried to focus on the room. At first it looked familiar. It looked like Josie's guest room. But Josie's guest room had a double bed, not a single. God, where on earth had I ended up? Couldn't be another woman, could it? No, I was definitely in a single bed. I looked around the room and noticed another single bed that was occupied. Now I was worried. Yes, you would be too! Did I get off with someone last night in my drunken state? But then, most dykes I know don't have two single beds. They would have a double for sure. As I began to get my focus back I realised I was in Josie's guest room. I then remembered her and Ivan doing it up. They decided to put two singles in, so that friends as well as partners could stay over. So, at least I knew where I was. The person in the other bed turned over and I realised it was Katie. I should have known that, as she's staying with Josie. Seeing her turned the jackhammer in my head off and at last I had silence. I watched her sleeping. She looked so lovely something in me shifted. Her hair was all dishevelled and her mouth was slightly open, but she still looked lovely. I wished Josie had kept the double bed. I would have loved to cuddle into Katie. Then I remembered why I'd got so pissed last night. I remembered Katie trying to seduce me. Remembered she was pregnant. Remembered I'd let myself fall for her. Why did I let it happen? I couldn't remember.

I got out of bed as quietly as I could and grabbed my clothes from the chair. Josie, my wonderful, thoughtful sister, had put a clean pair of panties with last night's clothes. I went into the bathroom and had a long shower. After getting dressed and cleaning my teeth I felt much more alive.

I went downstairs and into the kitchen where I could hear the radio playing.

"Good morning, Sis," I said, as I sat down at the table.

"Ah, the party animal is alive."

"Yeah, and I feel great ta," I said. "I'm starving, what you got to eat?"

"Typical, you down the liquid contents of a whole club and wake up as bright as the sun. I have one too many and I feel like shit."

"Are you hung-over then?"

"No, I'm not. Not today, I meant in the past. I was too busy keeping an eye on you to get pissed."

"Sorry, I didn't mean to spoil your evening."

Josie laughed. "You didn't. It was so much fun watching you. You entertained everyone in the club with your antics."

"Oh, God, what the hell did I do?"

"Don't panic, you didn't make a complete fool of yourself."

"But I did make a bit of a fool of myself?"

"Oh yes, it was great fun."

"What exactly did I do then?"

"Jess, hon, I'm only joking. All you did was ask every woman in the club to dance."

"Is that all?" I was relieved it wasn't anything more.

"You did flash your tits a few times, when your offer of a dance was refused. I think you were trying to show them what they were missing." Josie burst out laughing.

"Oh shit! Still I have got a nice pair of tits," I said joining in the fun of it. "Did any of the women I flashed change their minds?"

"No, they just took pictures with their camera phones." Josie laughed even more.

"Now I know you're joking. You'd never let anyone do that."

"True, but you did flash your tits a couple of times on the dance floor. I came over and stopped you doing it anymore."

"It'll probably come back in lurid detail later. I'll never drink again," I said, holding my head in my hands.

"Course you will, you always do. Everyone always does. We never learn."

"Yeah, you're right. Did I have a good time though?"

"Not sure. You were drinking for a reason. The last time you did that was when you split with Sue. So what was it last night?"

Uh-oh. Josie's brain cells were about to go to work.

"Does there have to be a reason?"

"Mmm, let's have breakfast then we'll talk."

What's great about a drunken night out is the fry-up the next morning. I loved it. The breakfast I mean. Well, I quite like having my fair share of alcohol as well. I just didn't like the bout of amnesia that sometimes followed.

"Sorry, Josie I've got to run. I'm due at the hair-dressers in half an hour."

I knew it was a lie and I'm sure Josie did, but she let it ride. I picked my keys and money from the table and headed for the front door.

"Jess, you don't cop out that easily." Josie followed me to the door.

"Who, me?"

"Yeah, you, I'll catch you later," she said, as I went out.

"I'm sure you will," I said, half under my breath.

"And don't mumble. It's rude."

I was halfway down the garden path and just raised my hand in a wave. I didn't dare look back.

Chapter Thirteen

I WAS STARVING. But I was also a coward and didn't want to talk to Josie, even though her fry-ups were wonderful. Still there was some compensation to walking home. It took me past the café so I could still indulge in my passion for the morning after plate of grease. I could also eat it in peace with no Josie trying to wheedle out of me what was wrong.

There was nothing wrong, of course. I was just hopelessly in love. In love with someone I couldn't have. God, I hope Katie didn't help Josie put me to bed. I'd woken up in one of Josie's giant T-shirts. She uses them to doss around the house during the summer, and to sleep in when she isn't well. Like me she slept in the nude the rest of the time. So if I'd been that drunk, Josie wouldn't have been able to manage on her own. Ivan wouldn't have been roped in as he'd have run a mile anyway. He's quite genteel really, but not a sissy, just sensitive to others, especially their feelings. I always thought he'd have been a great counsellor instead of a computer analyst. So it would have been Katie who would have helped. Well, that's unfair. She gets to see me all naked and vulnerable. I think she should repay the compliment. Well, perhaps not. I ate while I thought about everything. I needed to find out how long she was going to stay in England once the baby was born. Was she telling the truth when she said she and Bill were having problems? I wondered what those problems were. Mind you I had problems of my own to worry about. What was I going to tell Josie about why I got so pissed last night? How was I going to stand up to her scrutiny? Maybe I should just come clean and admit what had been going on. At least that way there'd be no lies to try and remember. I'm a lousy liar really. I always get caught out sooner or later. Josie can usually see right through me so I knew I was now on borrowed time. As soon as she comes round she's going to find me out. Ha. That's the answer. I'll be out. Get it? She'll find me out? Okay, maybe it's not that funny.

I paid for my breakfast and finished the walk home. It was now quite warm although the sky was very hazy, so no sunbathing today. Maybe I should keep my tits covered from now on, I laughed to myself.

It was only midday by the time I got home. A good time to get my cleaning done. It would only take a couple of hours. I usually liked to do it at the weekend, at least whenever I have the weekend off. I get it done nice and early, so I have the rest of the time for me. If I don't have a weekend off, I just do it as and when. I raced through the cleaning and was finished before two o'clock. Now I could have some me time.

I made myself a jug of fresh orange juice, lemonade and loads of ice. I went into the garden. It was nice sitting there even though it wasn't sunny. I lounged and relaxed then relaxed and lounged. It was great and I was off on Monday so I didn't have to worry about getting stuff ready for work. So I just lounged and relaxed some more.

I eventually decided to get something to eat. Relaxing can make you hungry. According to all the television cookery programmes, we should all eat haute cuisine. Not me, I eat old-fashioned stuff, bangers and mash, beef stew and dumplings. Don't get me wrong I like to eat the posh stuff too. I just can't be arsed with all that faffing around. It's like salad. When I do a salad, I just dump the whole lettuce leaves on the plate. I add tomato, beetroot, salad onions and all the other bits nicely arranged of course. I don't chop it up and mix it with a dressing. I just can't be bothered. No, you're right, I don't eat pasta. Yes, I know, I'm a philistine, but not everyone eats pasta. So I threw a few salad bits with some ham on a plate and went back out onto the patio.

I'd only just finished eating and was putting my plate in the sink, when I heard Josie's key in the front door. No escaping the talk now. I needed to keep my wits about me, although there was no point. I'd already decided to come clean, but only if directly asked. I wasn't going to offer anything.

"Hi, Josie, you want some coffee?" I shouted cheerily. I put my dirty plate in the sink and switched the kettle on.

"Yeah, please," Josie said, as she flopped on a chair at the table.

"You look hot and bothered. Do you want some orange juice and lemonade instead?"

Josie did look tired and worried, and I realised now wasn't a time for me to play games. I knew from past experience that when Josie is like this, it's best to keep on her good side. Don't make your usual flip comments, Jess. Mind you, sometimes I just can't stop myself doing it. Then I have to deal with the fall-out.

"That sounds lovely, yes please."

I made up a fresh jug with loads of ice and put it and two glasses on the table. Josie poured herself one.

"Okay, what is it you want to talk about?" I asked, pouring myself a glass.

Josie was quiet for a moment as if trying to get her thoughts in order.

"Jess, I know," she said, quietly.

"Know what?"

Well, I said I wasn't going to give anything up unless asked, didn't I?

"I know about you and Katie." It was as if she didn't want to have this conversation.

"Ah," I said, and waited for her to let me have it.

"I should have guessed it earlier, but I suppose I was too close to it."

"Look, Josie. It's not what you think. Nothing happened. I wouldn't. Not even me, honestly."

It was true, nothing did happen, apart from some serious snogging. I must have grinned at the memory.

"It's no laughing matter," Josie said, firmly.

"I know. I'm sorry." I felt like a naughty school kid in the headmistress' office.

There was silence and I could see Josie was struggling with something. I let it continue. I knew she'd tell me in her own time.

"I also know Katie's gay. I've known since we were at school," Josie said, after what seemed like hours.

She wasn't really telling me anything new, yet she was, but having it confirmed was good. It means the old gaydar is still up and working.

"Since when at school, and why didn't you tell me?"

"I didn't tell you because it wasn't my place to."

"But you're telling me now."

"Yes."

I waited. No further explanation was forthcoming.

"Since when did you know at school?"

"We were in year eleven and Katie wasn't her usual bubbly self. We talked on the way home. She told me she thought she was gay, and that she fancied one of the girls at school." Josie took a long drink. "I told her it was just part of growing up. We all go through having crushes on other girls or female teachers. It didn't mean anything, but none of this helped. She was distraught."

"I can imagine. She comes from a very strict Catholic family, doesn't she? Can't have been easy for her."

"Yes, and that was the biggest part of the problem. She couldn't reconcile feeling the way she did with her religious beliefs and upbringing," Josie said.

"Yeah, but we know Catholics who are gay and are okay with it."

"But are they really? How much soul searching did they have to go through before they reconciled it with the teachings of the Bible?" Josie asked.

"I don't know, is the honest answer."

"Exactly. Who knows what turmoil people go through, and Katie's no different. She's had a difficult time and now she's got to get it all sorted out. It's not going to be easy."

"I thought she had sorted it. She's married and expecting a baby."

"That's as may be. A lot has happened over the last year that she needs to put right. Especially regarding what happened with you."

"Look, Josie, we only kissed a couple of times. Nothing else, honestly. If you want to know, she threw herself at me a couple of times. I pushed her away. You'd have been proud of me."

"I know, Katie's told me everything," Josie said, wearily.

"Good, then you know I'm telling the truth."

"Yes, I know. Katie wants to come and talk to you, so she asked me to come and pave the way for her."

"Why didn't she just come round herself?"

"After yesterday she felt she wouldn't have got through the front door."

"Yeah, that's a point, I probably wouldn't have let her in."

"Jess, I want you to talk to her. Let her explain her actions. I just can't stand by and let the two people I care about most throw their lives away."

"What do you mean?"

"I know you're in love with Katie. I should have seen it earlier. I probably did, but it wasn't until I saw that photo of you both in Canada that it all fell into place."

"Ah, that," I said, resignedly.

"Last night after we put you to bed—"

"Please tell me Katie didn't help?"

"No and that was the strange thing that led me to talk to her finally. I managed to get you upstairs with Ivan's help. No, he didn't stay. Katie was still awake. You were flaked out and I needed help to get your clothes off. I asked her to help. I sat you up and asked Katie to take your top off. She made a feeble excuse and went downstairs."

"What did Katie say?"

"I asked her why she'd left me to it. I must admit she really pissed me off. She told me she didn't help because she didn't want to see you naked." Josie grinned at that.

I must admit I could see the funny side, but I resisted the temptation to make a quip.

"I told her I hadn't thought she was a prude. She went very quiet and eventually said she wanted you to be conscious when she saw you naked."

"Bit of a give-away, that."

"Yeah, I thought so too. So I asked her what she meant. She just blurted out that she was in love with you."

Josie's words hit me. My stomach lurched and I'm sure my heart missed a beat. Yes, I know, a bit dramatic. Katie was in love with me? That put a whole new complexion on things.

"Then she told me everything. I knew something was going on, but you managed to put me off the scent. That time at Nexus, when I caught you about to kiss Katie — "

"Yeah, I remember. I thought you were going to kill me."

It was good to be able to speak about all this and not to have to lie.

"Why were you so keen to keep me away from Katie?" I asked, remembering how protective Josie was.

"I wasn't trying to keep you away. I knew Katie was gay, but you were trying to shag your way through Croydon and beyond, if you remember."

"Yeah, that's true." I grinned at the memory. "Is that why you set me that challenge?"

Josie had the decency to look suitably caught-out.

"Yeah, it was the only way I could be sure you wouldn't make Katie one of your conquests. She deserves better."

"Josie, you make me sound like a love 'em and leave 'em bastard," I said, hurt at the implication. Mind you, she was right. I wasn't a very nice person at that time.

"Come on, Jess, you know what you were like. Also Katie is married. She had a hard enough time with all of that, without you complicating matters even more." Josie looked at me kindly. "Maybe subconsciously I thought this would happen. Maybe I wanted to stop it to protect you both."

"Protect us from what?"

"It's a mess isn't it, Jess? But it could have been a bigger mess without the challenge. What if you'd slept together?"

"For your information I didn't sleep with Katie because of me. It had nothing to do with that damned challenge! When she threw herself at me I could so easily have succumbed. However, I realised how much I cared for her and I couldn't. No, not couldn't, wouldn't."

"Are you sure it's not because it would have been too complicated?"

"No!"

"That it would have hurt too much when she went to New York with Bill?"

"No!"

"That it would have made it harder for you to get over Katie than it had been with Sue?"

"No! No!"

"Are you sure?" Josie's voice got louder as she pushed and pushed me with her words. And I knew some of them were true.

"No, it wasn't that."

"Don't lie to me, Jess. It wouldn't have been easy, would it?"

"No," I said quietly.

"Would it?" Josie was really in my face now. "Would it?"

I glowered at her. "No, it would have been fucking hard, but it wasn't just that," I shouted. I was really angry and couldn't stay seated. I got up and moved away from the table.

"Well, what was it then?"

"I—"

"Come on, what was it that stopped you? I really want to know."

"I love her!" I shouted. "Is that what you want to hear?"

"Yes, you moron." Josie got up and hugged me.

We held onto each other.

"It's a mess, isn't it?" I asked Josie after a few minutes of silence.

"Just a tad," she replied.

I sat trying to take it all in.

"So, will you talk to Katie?"

"Looks like I need to, doesn't it? This situation can't go on, we need to sort it out."

It would be strange seeing Katie, knowing how she felt.

"Shall I come over now?"

"No, it's all right. Katie's in the café down the road."

Josie saw the look on my face.

"I was sure you'd want to see her, so I thought it would be best for her to come over here. That way you can't run off and you won't chuck her out a second time."

Boy, Katie had told Josie everything.

"I was really angry. But at least I drove her back and didn't let her struggle on her own," I said, trying to retrieve the situation. "This time it's different, I won't need to throw her out. Because I need some answers. You'd better go and get her. I'll get some coffee organised, I think I'm gonna need it."

SO KATIE WAS in love with me. God did that sound good. But there was a long way to go before—before what?

I got up and put the kettle on to make some fresh coffee. I paced round the kitchen. I paced around the lounge. I tidied things away. I was nervous. More nervous than I was prepared to admit to anyone. I made myself sit at the kitchen table. I drank what was probably going to be the first of many cups of coffee.

Then I heard Josie's key in the door. This was it. I stood up nervously as first Josie came in followed by Katie.

We looked at each other and she gave me that smile. That was all it took and I was hooked into her so completely. I grinned inanely as she came over and kissed me. It was just a kiss on the cheek, but it was so soft and gentle. It was forgiving. It was — let's talk.

"Do you want some coffee?" I asked, once I'd regained my composure.

"Not yet. I've had enough to sink a battleship."

"Josie, do you want some?"

"Yeah, but I'll help myself. You two go into the lounge and talk. I'll stay out here."

We headed for the lounge. I sat in the big armchair while Katie took the sofa. We just looked at each other for what seemed like ages.

"Well, I suppose we'd better talk," I said, breaking the spell.

"Yeah, I suppose so."

"I suppose it's really down to me to try and explain why I've been behaving the way I have," she said, tentatively.

"Okay, I'm happy for you to start."

"I don't really know where though. It's been a hard journey for me over the last year or so." Katie spoke quietly.

I knew this wasn't going to be easy for her. But then, it wasn't my fault she'd got herself into this position, was it? Okay, so maybe I played a part.

"When I first discovered I was gay, it was the most awful thing for me. My family are strict Catholics, as you know. I was brought up Catholic and being gay didn't sit easily with that. I was terrified that if I told my parents how I felt, they'd disown me. I'd heard of lesbians for whom that had happened. They were very unhappy and I didn't want that."

"I guess I've been very lucky on that score."

"It's hard for some people to understand the way I've been brought up. The way I've been taught to live my life. But in some ways it's better to have that kind of structure than none at all. To be able to live with rules that enable you to live your life and to be kind to others. In this day and age we're losing that structure. Losing the family values that my parents taught me to live by. Sorry, if I sound like I'm preaching. Is any of this making sense?"

"In a way," I said.

"I could have just told my parents that I was gay. Could have gone off to live my life the way I wanted. But I couldn't take the risk I would lose their love."

"I can understand that."

Losing our parents had been the worst thing to happen to me and Josie, but at least we knew they were dead. With Katie she could have lost the love of her parents, but still been able to see them. She would be able to see them, but not be able to interact with them, not be able to share anything with them. Yes, I could understand that. If I had the choice, I don't know that I could have done it either.

"So I did what any good Catholic daughter should do. I got married and tried to give my parents grandchildren. I made my decision and would have stuck by it. Then I met you, Jess, and it all changed. I fell in love with you the moment I set eyes on you, if you can believe that?"

"Oh, I can believe that. I'm a good catch." I saw Katie look at me. Oops. "Sorry, I didn't mean to be flip. I just can't help myself sometimes."

"Don't be, it's one of the things I love about you," Katie grinned. She was beginning to relax.

"Why did you throw yourself at me, though?"

"I don't know. I knew your reputation and thought it would be easy. I wanted to sleep with you so much. I thought if you slept with me, we'd live happily ever after."

"No, I don't believe that."

"No, you're right. I didn't know what to do or how to do it. I'd seen a couple of lesbian movies and read a few novels. I wanted to get some idea of how to seduce a woman. None of it worked. It all went out the window and I just ended up throwing myself at you."

I laughed as I could see the funny side of it.

"I suppose it is funny. But at the time it was deadly serious. I wanted you so much I would have thrown myself at you at every opportunity. I was trying to send a message that I was gay."

"But you could have just told me."

"I didn't know how. Then I realised that you felt the same for me. I had a good think about what I was doing. I came to the conclusion that you were never going to do anything. The reason is you're a decent person underneath that supposedly brash exterior. That person wouldn't come between me and Bill, no matter what. You have morals. You may have spent a lot of time going to bed with every woman you could, but that was just to quench a pain."

"You've been talking to Josie, haven't you?"

"Yeah, she told me all about the challenge as well."

"It wasn't because of the challenge that I wouldn't sleep with you."

"I know. I could tell how much you wanted me. You just

wouldn't allow yourself to do anything about it."

"Okay, we're talking about us now. But what about Bill? How does he figure in all of this?"

I was worried. Maybe Katie and Bill were just having a glitch. Maybe she still wanted the best of both worlds. Was I being unkind? I suppose I was.

"Bill and I are finished." Katie sounded quite emphatic about it.

"Are you sure? Or are you just trying to justify being with me?"

"What do you mean?"

"Well, it just seems convenient that you say you and Bill are finished. Then you come back to England and say you're in love with me."

To say I was worried was an understatement. Maybe this was only going to be an interlude for Katie while she was back here. That once the baby was born, or she realised she couldn't be out, she'd go back to New York. Back to Bill and back into the closet. Katie looked hurt at my words.

"I'm sorry if what I'm saying hurts, but I need to be sure what's going on here," I said

"I can understand your concerns, so let me tell you what's led me here. When I realised I was gay I also realised it wasn't going to be easy. I was scared about what would happen if I told my parents. I kept quiet, as I said before, and did the right thing. It was right by what my parents had brought me up believing. Not right by the way I should be living. I worked hard at putting my unnatural feelings away. Behaving as I was expected to. Then I met Bill and it seemed the right thing to do, to get married. He was in love with me and I really liked him." Katie paused to gather her thoughts. "I need you to understand how serious I am."

"Okay."

"Everything was all right. We got on well and to start with we were happy. Well, Bill was probably happy. For me there was always something missing. Going to New York was Bill's idea. I think he knew something wasn't quite right. The job came up and he said it would be good for us both to get away and start afresh. Then before we were due to go I met you. It was then I realised that no matter how hard I put my real feelings to the back of my mind, they would always be there. I'm gay and there's nothing I can do about it. I'm no longer going to deny myself the opportunity to be happy."

I could feel the sadness Katie had been feeling for a long time. I got up and sat down next to her. I took her hand in mine and gave it a squeeze.

"Everything's going to be all right." Lame I know, but I couldn't think of anything else to say.

"Because of the pressure I was getting from my parents, Bill and society in general, I still went. It was quite exciting at first. Bill and I had a new lease of life. But that life wasn't really as a couple. His work was taking up a lot of time and I was left alone at home. Our sex life suffered, not that it was very good in the first place. I tried to enjoy it, but again I felt there was something missing. Bill started working later and later. I managed to make a couple of friends at the gym and that's when I also got myself a job. I spent quite a bit of time talking with Becki and Sydney and they helped with my dilemma. They knew I was gay as soon as they met me. They talked to me about my options but I still couldn't make the decision. Then I saw you again in Canada and I thought it was fate that we were meant to be together. But you were with Janey, or so I thought at the time."

"Yeah, sorry about that, but Janey and I are just good friends. We were lovers, but that never worked. We're much better at being friends. When we went to Canada it was easier to sleep in the same room, especially as Becki and Sydney were coming for the weekend. I was surprised to see you as well, but it was a nice surprise."

"I know all that now and I feel so silly when I think about it. When I got back to New York another surprise was waiting for me." Katie stopped.

The memory was obviously painful.

"What was that?"

"We got back earlier than expected and I went straight to the apartment."

I knew what was coming.

"Bill was just letting a very attractive woman out. He was still in his robe and it was obvious what had been going on. He just smiled at me and went inside. It was as if he didn't care that he'd been caught out. I followed him in and we talked. Well, Bill talked and I yelled. God knows why. I was surprised that I'd caught him out, but I don't think I was shocked. In fact, the more I think about it, I was pleased, even happy. Maybe I thought of it as the kick up the bum I needed to break free." Katie laughed. "Sounds like I was a prisoner, doesn't it? Maybe that's what I was, a prisoner in a prison of my own making. I ended up at Becki and Sydney's and they put me up until I could sort things out and come back to England. They were great. So supportive, especially when I found out I was pregnant."

"How did that come about?" I asked, then realised what a stupid question it was.

"Jess—"

"Sorry, what I mean is, you said your sex life wasn't up to much."

"True. We'd been out to dinner with Bill's company and both of us had quite a bit to drink. Bill started kissing me and I must admit I was enjoying it, probably the effects of the booze. By the time we got back to the apartment we were both very aroused. It wasn't making love. Not for either of us, I don't think. I know Bill needed sexual gratification and he so rarely got it from me. That's why he had an affair, I suppose. I don't blame him. I blame myself. I should have been strong enough to admit I was gay. It would have saved all the heartache. That was the last time we had sex and it was obviously then that I conceived. In some ways it's sad. A baby should be made from love, not need or necessity."

"At least it wasn't made from hate or because you were forced," I said, gently.

"True, but it's just unfortunate that our last sexual encounter ended up with me getting pregnant."

"Why do you say unfortunate? I thought you wanted kids?"

"If you remember, I said I wasn't sure."

"True, but how do you feel now?"

"I don't know. It's all such a mess. You have to agree, having a baby now is a complication."

"That depends on your point of view."

"I've made the decision to be honest with myself about who I am. I have the opportunity to go on a journey of discovery. Trouble is that I can't do that with a baby in tow." Katie gripped my hand.

I looked and saw a tear course down her cheek.

Chapter Fourteen

"I DON'T BELIEVE that for a minute. Nor do you. What is it you're really worried about?" I said.

"I'm worried about you."

"Me? Why on earth are you worried about me?"

"I want to be with you. I just don't know how you feel about being with me and a baby. I don't know if you'll want me enough to want to take on my baby as well."

I was quiet. I didn't know what to say. To be honest, I didn't know how I felt about Katie and a baby.

"Jess, please tell me what you think. I really need to know."

"I honestly don't know, Katie. I know I'm so totally in love with you that it shouldn't make a difference."

"But?"

"But I don't know. I need time to work it out in my head. Such a lot has happened in a very short space of time. I just can't take it all in."

It even sounded lame to me. What was my problem?

"Jess, you can have all the time you need. Just know that I love you, but I'm keeping my baby. I may not have been sure about having children, but now it's in here." Katie rubbed her tummy lovingly. "I'm keeping it."

"I wouldn't expect you to do anything else. What does Bill want?"

"Now there's a question. The bastard doesn't want anything to do with the baby," Katie said, bitterly.

"Jesus, why on earth not?" I was surprised. I thought Bill really wanted kids.

"The woman I caught him with is also pregnant. He feels that as I won't be living in America, it wouldn't be fair if he just flits in and out of the baby's life. He doesn't want to be a long distance father and he's happy with the child he'll see and bring up."

"Well, I don't want to side with Bill, but he's got a point. It wouldn't be fair on the child to have a father like that. Mind you, I wouldn't mind betting money is playing a part in his decision."

"You mean child support? Oh yes, that's definitely part of it. I told him to keep his money and keep out of my life. I can manage without him and I will."

I grinned at her. "I'm sure you will."

I looked deep into her eyes.

"You're gorgeous when you're angry."

"You're just gorgeous." She stroked my face. "Kiss me. I want to taste your wonderful kisses again."

I could do nothing but oblige, now could I? Besides I was desperate to kiss her and take away some of her pain.

Our lips met gently. Our tongues probing until we were kissing passionately, deeply, and nothing else mattered.

I pulled back slightly.

"Oh, Katie," I said against her mouth as I kissed her again.

Her hand reached for mine, placed it on her bump and held it there firmly. I pulled away from her kiss and looked into her eyes. She was pleading with me to leave my hand where it was. Then I felt it, the tiniest little kick against the palm of my hand. It was beautiful, wonderful. It was life. Katie looked at my reaction. My face must have shown what she hoped. She smiled and let go of my hand and I left it where it was. I kissed her so tenderly and then passionately. I was lost in that kiss, hopelessly lost.

"Sorry to interrupt," Josie said. "But I'm really tired. Jess, I'm gonna use your spare room. I can't be bothered to drive back home tonight." She did look tired.

"Josie, I'm really sorry, I didn't realise how late it was." I got up and gave her a hug.

"It's not that late, I'm just really tired. Ivan's away until Tuesday so I don't have to worry about him."

"Okay, I'll cook you a nice breakfast," I said.

"Make sure Katie gets back, won't you?" she said, as she went up the stairs.

"Yeah, will do," I shouted up after her.

"Jess, I don't want to go back to be on my own," Katie said when I sat back down.

"Does seem a bit daft. If I take you home, I might as well take Josie home seeing as how you're staying with her."

Katie laughed. "I think she's too tired to think straight. Please let me stay with you. I want to wake up with you."

I was unsure how I felt about sleeping with a pregnant Katie, although I would definitely be sleeping. It was a lot to take in.

"I don't know, Katie. I had this dream of sleeping with you. In it you weren't pregnant. I know it sounds selfish, but I can't sleep with you while you're pregnant. I don't think I'd be able to make love to you, knowing you're carrying Bill's baby."

"I knew it would end like this!" Katie cried. "I just knew it. I've ruined everything."

I pulled her to me and let her cry into my shoulder.

"No, you haven't ruined everything. I just need some time,

that's all."

"Yeah, I'm sorry. I did say I'd give you time and now I'm putting pressure on you already. I'm behaving like a spoilt brat."

"No, you're not. It's probably your hormones," I said, soothingly.

"Will you come to bed and just sleep with me then?"

I could do that. I knew I could do that. I wanted to sleep with Katie and I wanted to wake up with her. I wanted to hold her while she dropped off to sleep. I wanted to be with her. Well, at least one half of me did. The other half, well, the jury was still out.

I TOOK HER up to the bedroom and sorted out a couple of my big baggy T-shirts. I got a sheet out of the cupboard. It was still too hot to sleep under the summer duvet, but a bit chilly to sleep without a cover at all. I thought we'd sleep with the sheet loosely over the top of us. Being a good hostess, I let Katie use the bathroom first. While she was getting showered and changed I organised the bed. Not that it needed much organising. I had put new bedding on during my bout of cleaning earlier. I just put the quilt away, and then laid the sheet on the bed.

Katie came back looking very sexy in the baggy T-shirt.

"As it's so hot I think we should sleep with just a sheet covering us," I said.

"Yeah, it's all I sleep under myself when it's this hot. Since getting big it's too much to have a quilt."

"All right, you get settled and I'll get ready."

I went into the bathroom and showered. I put clean panties on as I didn't want temptation to get in the way. I put my baggy T-shirt on and surveyed myself in the mirror. Oh yes, dead sexy. Still, it would serve a purpose, although, from my point of view, Katie's bump would do that nicely.

Why did I feel like this? Maybe it's because it's not mine. I don't mean that as in I'd want to be the father. More as in if we'd been together and decided we wanted a baby. Then I would have been part of the process. I'd have to get this straight in my head if Katie and I were to make a go of it. Here I was, about to get in bed with the woman of my dreams, yet I didn't want to. But I knew I had to. I couldn't let her see I had more reservations. I went back into the bedroom.

Katie was already in bed and I climbed in beside her. No sooner had I got in than she moved and snuggled in close to me. It was really nice and I switched off the bedside light. There was just the streetlight shining through the curtains. Under other circumstances it would have been romantic.

"Will you kiss me before we go to sleep?" she asked, in the darkness.

"That's a silly question."

We kissed, but if I was getting aroused, I knew Katie would be too. I didn't want things to go that far, yet. I knew the bump would get in the way, and not just in the physical sense.

"We need to sleep," I said, pulling away.

"Yeah, I am tired now." Katie turned her back to me and we settled down in the spoons position. I remember a pregnant friend telling me once that she found it more comfortable to sleep on her side. It was okay for me for a short while, but I knew I would want to move soon. I find it more comfortable sleeping on my back. I listened to Katie breathing. When it became slower I knew she was asleep. I gently moved position so I was on my back. I kept close to Katie. I wanted to feel her against me. Lying in bed like this with Katie beside me, it was as if we'd been together forever. It was so natural and I just hoped she didn't snore.

Suddenly I got out of bed. I couldn't do it. I couldn't lay there with Katie feeling the way I did. God, what was I to do? I stood looking at her sleeping. Why the hell did I feel this way? I crept downstairs to the kitchen and made a cup of coffee. Fatal really, for when I did want to go to sleep I'd be too wired. But hey, I needed a bit of stimulation and I needed time to think about how I was going to play this. What was wrong with me? Being with Katie was all I'd ever wanted. All I'd waited for. Now it was here was I going to throw it all away? It all went round and round in my head with no real conclusion. What was it about Katie being pregnant that I couldn't handle? Or was I just making excuses? Was it because, as Josie had said, it really was too complicated?

Eventually I could think no more. I went quietly back to the bedroom and I saw that Katie hadn't moved. I climbed back in beside her, praying I'd be able to sleep. I lay quietly for a while and eventually dropped off.

THE NEXT THING I remember was Katie cuddling right up to me. She'd moved her position so she was facing me, her arm was across my chest. I felt her breath on my cheek, and opened my eyes.

"Morning," I said softly. "Did you sleep well?"

"The best I've had in ages. You're so nice to sleep with." She kissed me on the cheek.

We lay like this for a while just looking into each other's eyes. I think we'd have stayed like that forever if Josie hadn't come in with cups of tea.

"I did knock. I guess you didn't hear me," she said, smiling as she put the tray on the chest of drawers and handed us both a cup as we sat up in bed.

"Morning, Sis, did you sleep well?"

"I must have gone out with the light, I was so tired. I've only been up long enough to make the tea," she said, and promptly yawned.

We laughed at her.

"Maybe you need to go back to bed and sleep some more," Katie said.

"No, I'd better not. Otherwise I'll be there all day. Some of us have to go to work, you know. Ah, well, the joys of being a shift worker."

"And the joys of being pregnant," Katie said.

"You don't get sick in the mornings, do you?" I asked, alarmed that she might not make it to the bathroom.

"No, I've got through that bit, so I won't throw up in front of you," she said, grinning.

"I'm not worried about that. I thought you'd have been embarrassed, that's all."

"Can't be embarrassed when you're pregnant, not the way you get poked and prodded. Student doctors looking into every orifice. No time for embarrassment."

"Look, guys, I'm gonna have to leave you or I'll be late for work. Have a good day and I'll see you later," Josie said, and she left us to it.

A few minutes later I heard the front door open and close as Josie went off.

I looked at the clock. It was only seven thirty, much too early to get up. I finished my tea and slid back down in the bed. It was so comfy and I was feeling lazy.

"Jess, I have to go soon," Katie said, as she too finished her tea and snuggled into me.

"Why?"

"There's something I have to do and I'm not going to put it off any longer. I've put it off far too long as it is."

"What?"

"I'm going to spend some time with my parents, and I need to tell them I'm gay," she said, quietly. I could hear the strain in her voice. This was obviously not a visit she was looking forward to.

"How long will you be gone?"

"I don't know. I can't just drop the bombshell and leave them to it, can I?"

"No, I suppose not. Do you want me to come with you?" I offered, not really expecting her to take it up. This is something that can only be done on your own. It's something that has to be talked about with just your family. It would be hard enough for Katie knowing how she'd been brought up.

"No. I have to do this on my own, but thanks for the offer."

"That's okay, that's what friends are for."

"I'd hoped we were more than just friends." She looked at me searchingly.

A yawning chasm of silence opened up.

"Yeah, of course we are," I said, unconvincingly, dropping my eyes to the very interesting T-shirt I was wearing. I felt Katie's eyes on me, but couldn't bring myself to look at her.

Katie got out of bed.

"I've got to go."

With that she grabbed her clothes and went into the bathroom.

Shit, I could have been a bit more convincing. After all, I was dealing with a hormonal pregnant woman. What on earth was I thinking?

After a few minutes Katie came out, dressed in her clothes from yesterday.

"Katie, I—"

"It's okay, Jess. Maybe I'll see you when I get back," she said as she went downstairs.

I followed her down. "I'll drive you to Josie's."

"No, I'll walk, thanks." She opened the front door and was gone before I could change her mind.

"Well, that was well done, Jess. Nice one," I told the front door. What the hell was the matter with me? I'd spent the best part of a year pining for this woman. When I get the chance to be with her, I blow it. I hated the way I was feeling right now. I just couldn't get up any enthusiasm about Katie being here, about Katie wanting to be with me. She was all I'd ever wanted and yet I was pushing her away. I was being non-committal about any relationship we may or may not have. She was pregnant and everything had changed. There was a third person in the equation and I wasn't sure I could, or wanted, to deal with that.

Did this mean I didn't love Katie enough? Or did it mean I didn't love her at all? Was it all just a game, just the thrill of the chase and all that? Maybe it was just infatuation or lust. I was as confused as hell. It was time to call in the problem busters, Janey and Lucy. I gave Janey a call on her mobile and left a message. Unlike me, they were working. I'd forgotten it was Monday.

I went to the kitchen and put the kettle on for coffee. I went through the motions of cooking and eating breakfast, but I didn't really taste it. I washed up and had a long soak in the bath. I always find having a bath a good place to do some serious thinking. It's also a great place to relax. I put a soppy CD on, lit some candles and closed the curtains to shut out the world. After half an hour I was no nearer solving my problem. I was nicely wrinkled though, so I got out. I didn't want to shrivel up completely.

I'd just dried myself off and put shorts and a T-shirt on when the phone rang.

"Hi, girlfriend. I got your message. It sounds urgent. What's up?"

"Katie," I said.

"Ah, what time shall I come over?"

"Anytime you like. Will you bring Lucy?"

"Not if you don't want me to."

"Of course, bring her. I just want to know as I'll cook something and make sure we have enough to drink."

"Great, we'll be over at six then."

"Thanks, Janey."

"No probs. See you later."

That's what I like about good friends. They never tell you they've got something on to get out of being there for you. Even if Janey had something on, she'd put it off to help a friend in need. I was certainly one of those today.

I DECIDED TO go to the supermarket straight away. I'd get some chicken and a couple of bottles of wine for tonight. I would do a chicken salad, French bread, with strawberries and cream to follow. All washed down with some nice white wine. That way I wouldn't have to spend a lot of time cooking in the heat. The weather forecast warned of temperatures hitting the mid-eighties. It was great for sunbathing, especially in September. I did so love Indian summers.

By the time I got home it was feeling very hot. I made up some fresh orange juice, lemonade and lashings of ice. I sat in the shade on the patio, loaded up my CD player and just sat there thinking.

The same thing kept going round and round in my head. The baby. It always it came back to the baby. It wasn't the baby's fault. It hadn't asked to be brought into the world. It was a result of circumstance. I just couldn't see a way past that at the moment. Maybe with Janey and Lucy's help I'd be able to.

The only time I moved was to get a sandwich, replenish my drink and the CD player. I spent the whole day doing absolutely nothing. It was wonderful, or would have been if I'd not had to use the brain cells so much. In the end I read to take my mind off the loop it had got into. It did help as it put me to sleep. I woke suddenly and checked the time. It was nearly five. I needed to get organised in the kitchen before Janey and Lucy arrived.

Yes, I know, it's such a lot of work in banging a bit of chicken in the oven and washing a bit of salad. You're right, it didn't take long at all and I even managed a much-needed shower. The time I'd spent in the heat had made me all hot and sticky. By the time Janey and Lucy arrived, the table on the patio was laid and everything was ready.

"Come in, guys," I said, as I greeted them at the front door.

"Hi, Jess, how you doing?" Lucy asked. She gave me a kiss on the cheek.

"Not too bad," I lied.

"Yeah, we'll see about that," Janey said as she gave me a hug and a kiss.

"I thought we'd eat outside as it's still so nice," I said, ushering them through.

"Great, I love eating al fresco," Janey said.

"No, it's chicken salad," I said, seriously.

"Oh, very droll," Janey said, as she gave me a dig.

"Wine for you both?"

"Yes, please," Lucy said.

"No need to ask me," Janey said.

I poured three glasses of wine and took them out to the patio. Janey and Lucy were already sitting down and relaxing. They'd come straight from work, bless them.

"I'll just get the chicken if you'll uncover the other stuff for me," I said, as I went back to the kitchen.

Once I'd got the chicken sorted and we'd loaded our plates, we ate while we talked.

"So, girlfriend, tell me all," Janey said, forthright as ever.

"Well, you know Katie's back?" They nodded. "Well, she came round yesterday and stayed over," I said.

They both looked at me, saying nothing, but I could see the question in their eyes. I told them the whole story while we continued eating.

"So, what's your problem? It's what you've wanted since you first met Katie, isn't it?" Lucy asked, before Janey could say anything.

I nodded.

"It's the baby, isn't it?" Janey asked, incisive as ever.

I hadn't mentioned anything of how I felt about the baby.

"Yeah, it's the baby." I felt more than a little guilty.

"What is it about the baby that bothers you?" Lucy asked.

"I can't put my finger on it," I lied.

"I don't believe that for a second," Janey said, pouring more wine for us all.

"Did you and Katie make love last night?" Lucy asked.

"You know we didn't. I told you we just slept."

"Why was that, do you think?"

Janey smiled at Lucy's question. It was what she would have asked me. They really do suit each other, I thought.

"Come on, answer the question, girlfriend."

"I couldn't. I just didn't feel that way toward her. Maybe it was too soon after we'd admitted our feelings for each other."

"Crap!" Janey said forcefully. "You and I both know that's crap."

God, these two are like a couple of terriers with a bone. They're not going to let it go.

"Okay, its crap," I said.

"What's the real reason then?" Lucy asked, gently.

"I just didn't feel that way toward Katie." I was angry now. I was being forced to confront my feelings and I wasn't sure it was such a good idea now.

"All right, no need to get angry," Janey said, trying to calm me down. She poured more wine. "Drink some wine and chill. We're gonna sort this, so don't worry."

I picked up my glass and took a big mouthful. At this rate I was going to be well and truly pissed.

"When are you seeing Katie next?" Lucy asked.

"Don't know."

"What do you mean?" Janey asked.

"She's gone to her parents to break the news."

I told them what Katie's plans were.

"Will you talk to her while she's up there?" Lucy asked.

"We didn't make any plans to do so," I answered.

"You want to know what I think?" Lucy asked.

"What?"

"I think it's all too much hard work for you now. At first it was just you and Katie."

"And a husband," Janey added.

"True, but once he was off the scene, it would have been just the two of them, Janey. Bill was easy to get rid of in that sense. A baby isn't, nor should it be."

"So, what are you insinuating then, Lucy?" I asked.

"I'm not insinuating anything, Jess. What I'm suggesting is that maybe you want an easy life with no complications."

That hit home. There was an element of truth in what she'd said. I do like life to be uncomplicated and un-confrontational. God, I'd got a lot to think about.

"Okay, I can take that on board," I said.

"When does Katie come back?" Janey asked.

"She didn't say. I don't think she just wants to tell her folks and then run. In any case they'll want to spend some time with her. She is carrying their first grandchild."

"I suppose the only question you have to ask yourself is whether you love Katie or not," Janey said, to the point as usual.

"It may be the only question to be asked. But there are other things to consider," I said. And I wasn't sure if they were just obstacles I was deliberately putting in the way.

"Pray tell, girlfriend?"

"Right, what happens once the baby's born?" I asked.

"I'd have thought that was easy. You have your work cut out for you," Lucy answered.

"Well, that's gonna be a problem isn't it? With me working shifts I'll never get any sleep or any time alone with Katie."

"You really are trying to put obstacles in the way, aren't you?" Lucy asked.

"No, just pointing out the blindingly obvious."

"How do you think other people cope?" Janey asked.

"I'm not other people. Look, it is too complicated."

"Life sometimes is. You can't have it easy all the time," Lucy said, gently.

"And yeah, I don't know if it's what I want anymore."

"Right, like we're gonna believe that. You need to have a serious talk to yourself, girlfriend. Get your act together before you lose everything you ever wanted."

"We'll leave you to it. You know where we are if you want to talk some more," Lucy said.

"Yeah, thanks guys. See you later." I let them out.

After Janey and Lucy had gone, I sat with the dregs of the wine and my thoughts. What was I to do about this mess? I'd spent all this time thinking about how it would be if Katie and I ever got together. Now I had the opportunity I couldn't, or wouldn't, take it. What the hell was the matter with me? Why couldn't I just accept that at long last Katie had chosen to be with me?

I cleared up the dinner things and washed up, my thoughts hounding me as I tidied up. I really didn't want to go to work tomorrow, but I couldn't get out of it. Maybe it would be a blessing in disguise. At least with work to occupy my mind I'd have less time to think about Katie and this mess. Why was it a mess though?

I went to get some more wine but realised I'd had my quota. I was working tomorrow so I swapped it for a Diet Coke. I sat thinking hard.

Again that question, why was it a mess?

It was one I couldn't seem to answer. I loved Katie. That much I was sure of. Katie loved me, so in theory it should have worked out fine. Then baby makes three and this was the problem, the baby. It always came back to the baby. Why did that bother me so much? Was it because I knew I wasn't responsible enough to bring a child up? Or was it because it was Bill's baby and I really didn't like Bill? No, that was too petty even for me, and too easy. The baby hadn't asked to come along. It was the innocent party in all of this. I wasn't ready to be a mum and it was too soon to be having a baby, for me that is. It had hit me hard when I'd seen Katie pregnant. She couldn't be exclusively mine. She had to be someone else's as well. That someone else was the baby. What it really comes down to is that I'm jealous.

Okay, Jess, now you've come to this momentous conclusion, what are you going to do about it?

Yes, that was the big question. What the hell was I going to do about it? I think I hurt Katie. No, of course I don't think I'd hurt Katie. I knew I'd hurt Katie. At the time of saying it, I think I wanted to hurt her. I wanted to punish her for getting pregnant. I wanted to get back at her for bringing a third person into the relationship. Well, hardly a relationship. We'd only just started out. Now it looks like it's finished before it's even begun.

I wondered if Katie had left for her parents' yet. I could give Josie a ring.

Chapter Fifteen

"HI, JOSIE, HAS Katie left for her parents yet?" I asked when she picked up the phone.

"Ah, Jess. I'm coming over." With that the phone went dead.

I returned the phone to its cradle and made some coffee. I was glad I didn't start work until tomorrow afternoon. It looked like it was going to be a long night.

I heard Josie's key in the front door and braced myself for the onslaught.

"What the hell were you thinking of?" she asked, as she flew into the kitchen.

"What—"

"Katie was in a right state when I got back from work. It took me ages to calm her down."

"Look, Sis, I'm going through a bit of a crisis at the moment."

"You are? And what about Katie?" Josie plonked down on one of the kitchen chairs. "She's the one who's going to have a baby she now says she doesn't want."

That blew my mind.

"Why doesn't she want the baby?"

"I would think that's bloody obvious. It's because she knows you don't want it. She knows you don't want her and the baby."

"I never said anything to her."

"You didn't have to. She's not stupid. She'd rather not have the baby, but have you. She'd make that choice for you." Josie got up and poured out the coffee.

"But when we were talking she said she was going to keep the baby."

"That was before you had your—bit of a crisis. Fortunately, I got her to see reason. She was just having a knee jerk reaction to the jerk she'd just left."

She was right. I was behaving like a right idiot.

"So, has she left to go to her parents?"

"Yes, she went before lunch. She should have arrived by now. She said she'd call to let me know she'd arrived safely."

"Can you tell her I'm sorry? Ask her if I can call her?"

"I'll try. The last thing she said to me was that she didn't want to see or speak to you again. I'm sorry, Jess. I really think you blew it."

I sat and took in Josie's words. It was then that it hit me. I did want Katie and the baby. Knowing I had lost them brought me to my senses, but was it too late?

"Are you sure she won't talk to me?"

"That's what she said, and I can't say I blame her. She put everything on the line for you. She's gone to tell her folks she's gay, all for you. Well, not for you now, for her."

"It should always be about her," I said. "She should tell her folks because she wants to be honest with them, not because of me."

"I told her that and she's still going to tell them. But now it's because she wants to."

"I've made a mess of this, haven't I?"

"You sure have. I just don't know where you're coming from on this," Josie said, completely bemused.

"I didn't want a third person in the relationship. I didn't want Bill's baby in the relationship."

"I know you don't like Bill, but isn't that taking it a bit too far?"

"I know, I know. You don't have to tell me. I spent some time talking with Lucy and Janey and thinking about all that's happened. It's only now with you telling me she doesn't want to see or talk to me again, I realise what a fool I've been."

"Oh, and now you want Katie?"

"I do."

"That's convenient, isn't it?"

"What do you mean?"

"Well, Katie tells you she doesn't want to see or talk to you again. Suddenly you make up your mind what you want."

I didn't get what she was saying. I can be a little bit slow on the uptake sometimes.

"I'm sorry, you've lost me."

"I'm not surprised Katie wants nothing to do with you. It would seem you only want her when you can't have her."

Boy, did that one sting and I never saw it coming. But that's the trouble with Josie, she can put the boot in where it really hurts. Was she right? I really would have to think about that one.

"I can't talk to you right now, I'm too angry. You've really let yourself down this time, Jess. I must say I'm very disappointed in you." Josie got up and went out.

I sat at the kitchen table open mouthed for a few minutes, before I realised she'd actually gone. Yes, definitely slow on the uptake at the moment.

Only want her when I can't have her. Was that it? Did I just revel in the challenge of chasing something I knew I could never have? And if there was a possibility that I could have it, was I going to put obstacles in the way so I still couldn't have it? Did I only want Katie when I knew I couldn't have her? Now Katie didn't want anything to do with me, I wanted her. Was that the answer? Was I forever going to chase what I couldn't have? Did it all go back to Sue? Once she dumped me I wanted her more because I knew I couldn't have her. Perhaps that's why I went on my one-woman shagging spree. I wanted what I couldn't have. Well, to be truthful, I could have and did have all those women. Ooh bragging or what? But deep down I didn't want them. Maybe that's where it all started. I thought I had the perfect relationship. When Sue left, she took that away. Therefore, the perfect relationship was not there to be had. It was unavailable and I made sure it was never available by sleeping around and convincing myself I'd never have it.

Then along comes Katie and that's when my plans to spend my life as a poor-hard-done-by fall into a heap of shit. I fall in love with her and I want her. Is it because I know I can't have her because she's straight, married and very unobtainable but I've got to try anyway? Trouble is she's not straight and suddenly she's not going to be married anymore. Now she's available, now I'm scared. Now I have to put my money where my mouth is. Ha, but I can still get out of it. I can still feed my desire to go for the unattainable. She's pregnant. I can't have that and I can't get involved with her now. She's unattainable because I made her so. Because I need to get that buzz, yes, that's a part of it. But I could still have that buzz in a relationship, couldn't I? I did with Sue, so I could again. Then maybe it's that big word, commitment, I'm afraid of. Well not the word itself, of course, just what it stands for. I wouldn't get that buzz with Katie now though. She'd blown me out and I couldn't blame her.

I finally exhausted myself with all the thinking I was doing. I had to sleep. I tried, but it was a very fitful sleep with some very strange dreams.

BY THE TIME I'd finally decided I wasn't going to get any more sleep it was time to get up anyway. I made some coffee, egg and bacon for breakfast. I felt I needed a good amount of cholesterol to get me through the day. I'd still got to face work after the long weekend I'd just had off. Considering hardly any of that time was spent in restful pursuits, I knew I was going to suffer.

I sat and read one of the Sunday magazines. Yes, I know it's now Tuesday, but they don't have a 'read-by' date. An article I saw gave me food for thought. It could be my way to get back into Katie's life and maybe back into Josie's good books. I made some notes and decided to investigate further.

I was busy doing this when I heard Josie's key in the door. I quickly put the magazine away and hid my notepad. I didn't want Josie to know anything about what I had in mind.

"Hi, Sis, you want some coffee?"

"Yes, please."

"Why aren't you at work?" I asked realising it was a workday for Josie.

"I had a dentist's appointment and thought I'd take the whole day off. I'm owed a bit of time so I took it."

"Don't blame you, sounds good to me."

"Jess, I'm sorry about yesterday. I went off on one and you know me, once started I can't stop." She grinned.

"Yeah, you're a bit like a steam roller. It's okay, you were right."

I caught Josie's look of disbelief and asked, "What?"

"I can't believe you actually agree with me." Josie sounded incredulous at what I'd admitted to.

"I've been doing a lot of thinking and had very little sleep because of it, I might add. The conclusion I've come to is you were right. I've been a selfish idiot. I was more concerned with me than anyone else. I just hope it's not too late to make amends where Katie is concerned."

"I don't know about Katie. I think you hurt her very deeply with your attitude. She's going to take a lot of convincing."

"Yeah, I know it was stupid. Her hormones must be all over the place. She didn't need me being flip about whether we were more than friends. Trouble is, at that moment I couldn't see the wood for the trees. It happened so quickly. I felt like I was trapped, like I'd made a commitment and couldn't get out of it. I know I hadn't, but the way Katie and I'd been with each other over the last year, she must have thought I'd make that commitment."

"She said as much to me. I just didn't understand where you were coming from with all of this."

"I'm not sure myself. I just know that for a long while, ever since Sue, I've put obstacles in the way of me having another relationship. I thought Sue took away from me the chance to have a long-term relationship, so subconsciously I put barriers up. It then became a challenge to get what I couldn't have, until Katie came along. Before that, I knew I could go out with any woman and have my wicked way with her. I know, not a good thing to put on the CV. But when Katie came along that all changed. She couldn't be had because I thought she was straight and because she was married. I suppose I thought she was safe to love 'cos she wouldn't love me back. I could project my feelings onto her safely. She was off limits, but it didn't stop me." I took a breath, I knew I was gabbling. "But then it became obvious that she did want me. Now I have to make a decision. Do I want to go for it, or do I just knock it on the head because now the buzz I was getting has gone?"

"Jesus, Jess, you have been doing some thinking, haven't you?"

"I told you I didn't sleep much. Trouble is I don't know what to do."

"How do you mean?"

"Will you help me get Katie back?"

Josie sat thinking and looking at me. What was taking so long? Surely all she had to do was agree, then everything would be all right. I knew Katie would listen to Josie.

"No," Josie replied at last.

"What?"

"No, I won't help you get Katie back. You have to do this yourself. You've had it too easy with women up to now. You need to learn what it's like to really fight for something you want. You need to know if it's what you really want before you start to fight. Katie doesn't need to go through losing all she's ever wanted, again."

Well, that told me. Why was she being so unkind? It was so unlike Josie not to want to help me.

"Well, if you're gonna be like that–"

"I am, and don't take that tone. You know I'm right. If I smooth the way, then you have done none of the hard work. It will come too easily. You won't appreciate what you've got that way."

God, I hate it when she's right.

"Will you at least give me Katie's parents address?"

"She made me promise not to do that, so I can't give you their address."

"I'll email her then."

"There's no point. She's not using her email for that very reason."

"How the hell do I get in contact with her?"

"Write a letter and I'll send it for you. That much I'll do."

"Oh, that's big of you."

"Jess, don't. Sarcasm is the lowest form of wit."

"Sorry."

Why do I always feel like I'm the child and she's the mother? Maybe it's because I behave like a child sometimes. "I'll write one when I get back from work tonight and get it to you tomorrow."

"Fine, I'm writing to her myself tonight, so I'll keep my envelope open to put yours in."

"Will Katie reply to my letter, do you think?"

"I honestly don't know, Jess. She was very hurt by the cavalier attitude you displayed after she stayed the night with you."

"So I could be on a hiding to nothing?"

"Put it this way, you've got your work cut out for you," Josie said. "Let me ask you something. Are you really serious about you, Katie and the baby? Or is it just the fact that you can't have her?"

"I've been asking myself that all night."

"What's the answer then?"

"I don't know. What do you mean I can't have her? Do you know something?"

"No, at the moment I have no idea what's in Katie's mind. All I do know is that she doesn't want you coming up and making a scene. She's going to have a hard enough time telling her parents she's gay. It's not going to be easy to live a gay life and keep her baby."

"Oh shit! I've really blown it, haven't I?"

"I think maybe you have," she said, and put her hand on mine.

"I've been such a fool. I thought the baby would come between us and it has, because I've made it come between us. I just wanted it to be me and her. When I saw she was pregnant it was quite a shock. I think it was at that moment I began to feel differently toward her. Before, I would have gone to bed with her in a flash. But I just couldn't see myself making love to her with the bump."

"Why? She's still the same person."

"I know that. Maybe I would have felt differently if I'd been part of the—let's get pregnant—process. If she and I had been together and then decided to have a baby between us. Oh, I just don't know any more."

"Maybe you'd better write this all down and send it to her. It can't hurt and you owe it to both of you to give it a try, if it's what you really want."

"You know what, Josie? Sitting here talking this over with you, I realise it's what I've always wanted. I'm just being selfish in wanting it to be on my terms. I can't have it my way so I won't have it at all? Rubbish. I can have it all. I just hope it's not too late."

"So do I, Jess. You two are so right together. I know that much."

Must be her sixth sense kicking in again and this time I'm praying it's right.

"Okay, got to go and cook some dinner. I promised Ivan a nice roast for when he came home from work." Josie got up and moved to the front door.

"Yeah, I need to get ready for work as well. I'll write a long letter tonight, putting down everything. I just hope Katie reads it." I gave Josie a big hug and saw her out.

As I got ready for work I thought about what I'd write to Katie. I suppose I'd have to lay my heart on the line to get anywhere. I needed to let her know that I'd been a fool to let her go without telling her how I felt. I really hoped it wouldn't be too late. I had no idea how long she was going to stay at her parents, or whether she'd be back before the birth. I knew Josie was Katie's birthing partner and suddenly felt jealous. I wanted to be Katie's birthing partner. I wanted to see the baby born and to hold it after. It would be a way of affirming my feelings for Katie and the baby. Maybe Katie would make arrangements to have the baby while she stayed with her parents.

CHRISTMAS HAD COME and gone, so had the New Year and I'd hardly realised it. I was working most of the time, so I didn't get involved in any of the celebrations.

I felt really miserable. I'd written to Katie nearly every week and had no reply from her. Not even a — fuck off I never want to hear from you again! That would have been something. Josie wasn't giving anything away. If she'd discussed me with Katie, she wasn't telling me. I just wish I knew, one way or another, what was going on. I'd made myself a mental timetable. I knew from what Katie had said that the baby was due at the end of December. I would give it until the end of February before I gave up hope and wrote it off. I owed it to myself to give it that long. That would give Katie time to get used to having a baby around and her hormones to get back to some semblance of normality. Maybe then she would get in touch and we could talk things over.

I really missed Katie and knowing her absence was due to my insecurity, and the fact that I was a downright bitch, didn't help. I kept myself busy so the time had gone quite quickly, and my project was nearly finished. I just had one more thing to get and it was all done. It'd taken me the best part of two months to do, but gave me a focus, especially over the Christmas and New Year period. While I was doing it I managed to keep my thoughts away from Katie.

I went upstairs and checked on my handiwork. As I looked round, I noticed a couple of things I didn't remember buying. But then I'd bought a lot of stuff over that last couple of months so I'd probably forgotten.

I could hardly believe it was nearly the end of January. Where had all the time gone? What had I done with my life since meeting Katie? Pined most of it away, but that wasn't really true. I had redecorated the little room and the guest room. I'd hardly been out at all during the time since Katie went to her parents. No, I didn't wait with bated breath by the phone. Well, maybe I did for the first couple of weeks. Then I thought I would waste away if I didn't move. Only kidding, but I realised I was being a complete prat and needed to get back on track, hence the decorating. At least it was a good excuse not to go out.

"JESS, HOW NICE to see you. We'd almost forgotten what you look like," Lou said.

"Oh, very funny. I've been busy decorating the other two bedrooms, if you must know."

"Excellent. When can I come and stay?" Mel asked.

"Ha, I'm still not finished, so not yet."

"When will you be finished?" Lori asked.

Lisa laughed. "Bet it's just an excuse not to come out."

"Yeah, you've become a boring old fart lately," Shelley said.

"Sorry about that, guys. I really am decorating, but I'm nearly finished. Then I'll have more time to go out with all you rabble."

I ducked as several beer mats were thrown at me.

"Hey, no need to get violent."

I picked up the mats and put them back on the table. It was great to be out with the gang. I'd missed it. I should remember that next time I'm feeling sorry for myself.

"Right, who wants a drink?" I asked, and went to the bar.

Mel joined me.

"How are you, really?" she asked, getting straight to the point.

"Yeah, I'm not bad. Do you know about Katie?" I asked, not sure what Josie had told anyone.

"I spoke to Josie when Katie went off to her parents. I thought it was a bit sudden so I asked Josie what was going on," Mel said. "Josie needed someone to talk to and we had a long chat about what happened between you and Katie."

"I made a mess of it. I think I really blew it and I still haven't had any reply from Katie. I guess I may have to accept that she's not interested."

"You've changed," Mel said. She looked at me closely. "There's something different about you."

"Yeah, I've grown up."

"Not too much, I hope."

"No, definitely not too much."

We took the drinks back to our table. There was silence, which is not normal for our gang.

"What?" I asked.

"There's something different about you," Shelley said.

"Yeah, we've decided you've got a secret woman," Lou chimed in.

"Not that again," I said, exasperated.

"Yeah, that again. Come on, who is she?" Lori asked.

"What time have I had to meet anyone? I've been too busy decorating and working." I took a long drink of my lager.

"I bet Josie knows. Where is she?" Lisa asked.

"She's gone out with Ivan for a romantic meal," I said.

"What about Lucy and Janey? I bet they'd know," Shelley said.

"They've gone to see Lucy's mum for the weekend," Mel said.

"No one knows anything 'cos there's nothing to know." I tried to sound convincing.

"Oh, right, like we believe that," Lou said.

"Oh, I give up," I said, throwing my hands up in the air.

Lisa laughed. "Ha, so there is someone."

"No, no there isn't. Now please drop it." I was beginning to get angry.

"Okay, don't lose it," Shelley said.

"Come on, chill everyone, we're getting way too serious," Mel said, trying to lighten the mood.

"Yeah, let's party," Shelley said, and dragged Lou onto the dance floor.

Chapter Sixteen

SO HERE I am, just checking the decorating and hoping something will happen on the Katie front before my February deadline. I know it sounds callous, but it's the only way I know how to protect myself from further hurt. It was Janey's idea...

"I just don't know what to do," I said to Janey and Lucy. We were having lunch at Janey's. Well, it was now Janey and Lucy's since Lucy had moved in. Next step was buying a place together after Christmas.

"So Katie hasn't replied to any of your letters yet?" Janey asked.

"No, and I've sent one every week since she left."

"Maybe she needs time," Lucy said.

"Yeah, I thought that for the first couple of weeks. I poured my heart out in those letters, hoping I could explain how I felt and that she'd understand," I said. "I hoped that after a couple of weeks she'd reply."

"Well, maybe she didn't understand. I mean, when you look at it, you spent all this time wanting to be with her. When you get the chance you change your mind. It must be a bit confusing to say the least," Janey said.

"I really don't know why Katie being pregnant should have had an effect on me," I said.

"Maybe its tangible evidence that she was still sleeping with Bill," Lucy said.

"More that it was a bloke."

"Janey!" Lucy said.

"Well, I'd be pissed off if the woman I fancied was sleeping with a bloke," Janey said. "Especially when she's so obviously gay."

"Hey, guys, no fighting now."

Actually these two didn't fight, which was surprising. Janey can, at times, try the patience of a saint.

"It was a shock seeing Katie pregnant. Suddenly everything changed and I didn't know how to deal with it."

"And you do now?" Lucy asked.

"Oh, yeah for sure," I replied emphatically. "I'd just ask her to come and live with me."

"What about the baby?" Janey asked.

"Of course, the baby as well."

"Jess, I'm sure it'll all work out all right, but you have to protect yourself," Janey said seriously.

"How do you mean?"

"Well, how long are you gonna wait? I'm sure it's crossed your mind," Lucy said.

"Yeah, it has. So how long do I wait?"

"Only you can decide that. But you should allow time for the birth and the hormones to get back to normal. Then a bit more for luck," Lucy said.

"Maybe give her space by not writing for a while," Janey said.

"What you say makes sense. I'll give it some thought."

IT WAS GOOD advice from Lucy and Janey. All I had to do was stick to whatever decision I made, which was hard. Well, the letter writing part of it. I'd enjoyed writing to Katie, even though I wasn't getting any replies. I didn't even know if she was reading them, but none of that mattered really. It was good for me to write down how I felt and try to explain things. Like why I went from being a woman who really wanted to make love with her, to giving her the cold shoulder. It gave me a chance to think about what had happened and to think about my feelings. Why was I such an idiot? Would I ever get a second chance? I hoped so. And if I did, I'd make sure I didn't squander it.

I stretched out on the sofa. I deserved a rest. I'd finally finished the decorating. The place still had the smell of fresh paint, but it wasn't too bad. Aromatic candles work wonders.

The best thing was that as of now, I was on holiday. I wasn't going anywhere, just taking each day as it came. If I fancied jumping in the car and driving off, that's what I'd do. There were some great country pubs for lunch and yes, I can do soft drinks.

As usual, for a Sunday evening, there wasn't much on the television. I surveyed my collection of DVDs and decided on *Imagine Me and You*, a great feel-good film and I needed to feel good at the moment.

I made myself a sandwich, poured a glass of lager and settled down. It was great knowing I had a week off. I could really unwind.

The film was about halfway through when the doorbell rang. I looked at the time. It was still early at just gone seven o'clock. I stopped the film and got up to answer the door. I really hate being disturbed, especially when I'm in the middle of a good film. Yes, I do know what the pause button is for.

I opened the door to find Katie! She handed me a bundle and

hooked a bag over my shoulder.

"Take, Molly, I've got to get some stuff from the car," she said, as she turned and walked down the path to her car.

I stood open mouthed 'til she returned.

"Jess, close your mouth, there's a bus coming," she said. "Take Molly inside, I don't want her out in this air."

She was right, it was a little misty and cold.

"Oh, yeah, right." I suddenly realised the bundle was Molly and that Molly was Katie's baby. I know this because Katie no longer had a bump. Yes, I know, I can really catch on quickly.

Katie had a large bag over her shoulder and a large case on wheels she was pulling behind her. Now, correct me if I'm wrong, but I didn't think babies needed that much stuff.

I took the bundle and went into the lounge while Katie closed the door and dropped her bags in the hall. Bundle suddenly moved, making me jump. God, I nearly dropped it. No not it, Molly. I pulled the blanket open so I could see her. She was so small. I hardly felt any weight in my arms at all. I looked down into the eyes of the bundle and was lost immediately.

"She smiled at me," I said, excitedly.

"No, it's just wind," Katie said, taking her jacket off. She threw it on the armchair.

"Are you sure?"

"Yeah, she's too young to see anything much but shadows."

I was disappointed.

"Shall I take this blanket off her?"

"Sure, are you all right with handling her?"

"I'll try not to drop her."

"Oh you're so funny."

I gently removed the blanket. Once I'd done this I could see how small she really was.

"How old is she?" I asked.

"Seven weeks and two days."

"I take it she was early then."

Molly started to wriggle as I held her.

"Nearly three weeks. Give her to me. She needs a feed."

Katie took Molly and the bag that was still on my shoulder and sat down on the sofa.

"Do you want a drink?"

"I'd love a coffee please." She unzipped the bag as I went out to the kitchen to make the coffee. I was still a little stunned. Katie had walked in like nothing was wrong between us. Maybe it would be all right after all.

Molly, eh? It was a nice name and she was a nice baby. No, not nice at all. Gorgeous! Honestly, she really was. Her mum wasn't bad either.

I poured two mugs of coffee and went back into the lounge. Katie was in the middle of getting a bottle for Molly.

"Can you put this in the microwave for a few seconds, please?" she asked, proffering the bottle to me.

"Yeah, sure. Do you want a jug of cold water in case it's too hot?" I've seen mums ask for it in restaurants.

"Yes, please."

I put the mugs on the coffee table and did as was told. Katie certainly had this mum thing off pat.

I returned with the heated bottle and a jug of cold water. I handed the bottle to Katie who shook it to get a couple of drops onto the back of her hand.

Katie grinned. "Hmm, not bad for a beginner."

"I have hidden talents."

"Do you want to feed her?"

"No, you carry on. I'll watch." I was a bit nervous about this whole feeding baby thing, I guess.

I watched as Katie fed Molly. She looked so at home, a real earth mother. It filled my heart to see it and I wondered why I'd become so tied up with the worry that the baby would come between us. Finally, Katie put Molly up to her shoulder to do the wind thing and Molly obliged. Amazing really, in a couple of years Katie would be telling Molly off for doing it.

"Can you hold her while I sort her night bottle out?" Katie handed me Molly before I could reply.

Night bottle?

I looked down at Molly, who was now sound asleep in my arms.

"Shall we take her up to her room?" Katie asked, returning after a few minutes.

"How did—Josie! Now it all makes sense," I said. "I thought there were a couple of extra things I didn't remember buying."

I got up gently so as not to wake Molly.

"Can you manage?"

"Of course, she's as light as a feather. Come on. I'll go up first. That way if I fall I can land on you."

"Oh, you are so hilarious."

I stood outside the bedroom door.

"Molly, this is your room. I hope you like it." She was asleep, so I doubted she heard me, but what the heck.

I opened the door and switched the light on.

"Oh, Jess, it's beautiful, really beautiful."

"It's not bad, though I do say so myself."

I'd done the room out Pooh Bear style. The walls were a lemon yellow so it was nice and bright. The ceiling was a pale blue to represent the sky, with a couple of fluffy white clouds. The light was within a cut-out sun shape for daytime. At night there were quite a few tiny lights in the sun shape so that it looked like stars. The carpet was a nice green to represent the grass and I'd even painted some tall grass up from the skirting onto the walls. There were a couple of paintings, one of Pooh and his honey pot and one of Pooh and Tigger. The cot was white and the solid ends had Pooh Bear on them. I'd put a white shelf unit in against one wall and next to it a table for changing Molly's nappy. The cot bedding was Pooh, of course, and there was a wooden rocker with nice cushions in the corner.

I went over and closed the plain yellow curtains. I thought Pooh-patterned curtains would have been over the top.

"There's even somewhere to sit while you feed Molly," I said, indicating the rocker.

"The pictures are great. I didn't know you were an artist."

"I'm not. I used an over-head projector and acetates. I just drew round the outline and then painted it in."

"Well, it's still good. The room is so bright and cheerful."

"I've fitted a dimmer switch so you can adjust the amount of light in the room at night," I said. "The starlight is on a timer and it sparkles."

"Wow, an electrician as well. Is there no end to your talents?"

"No, I had to get someone in for that," I said before realising I was being teased.

I put Molly in the cot and covered her up.

Katie gave her a kiss before I pulled the side up. I was glad I'd oiled everything.

"Let's get our coffee," I said, as we went downstairs. "Do you want anything to eat?"

"No, I'll be fine until breakfast."

Breakfast? Night bottle? I got the message!

We went into the lounge and sat on the sofa.

"Well, this is unexpected."

"I know. I just wanted to arrive unannounced. I thought there'd be less chance of you saying you'd be out."

"I'd never do that. I've been waiting to hear from you."

"I'm sorry I never wrote back to you. I wasn't sure how I felt. Well, I was sure how I felt about you, but I was so hurt by what happened."

"That was my fault. I didn't know how to react to your pregnancy. It really threw me and I don't know why. I am so sorry I hurt you."

"And how do you feel now?"

"I feel like a prize idiot. If only I'd told you then how I felt. How worried I was that the baby might have come between us. We could have saved all this time and unhappiness." I couldn't look at her.

"Jess, it's okay. I do understand. I also think things had to play out the way they did."

"How do you reckon on that?"

"It gave me time to really think about what I wanted. Even as I went up to my parents, I wasn't sure if I would tell them or not. If I couldn't be sure about us then maybe I didn't have to say anything at all," Katie said, and took hold of my hand.

"But surely you'd have told them for you, not me?"

"You're right, of course. It had everything to do with you, in that you were the reason I couldn't put these feelings behind me anymore. But it also had nothing to do with you whether or not I would tell my parents."

I did understand what she was saying and I was glad she was honest with her parents.

"How did your mum and dad take it?"

"I didn't tell them straight away. I spent some time with them and talking about breaking up with Bill. They weren't happy about that."

"But surely they didn't expect you to put up with his affair and other child?" It beggared belief that they would expect her to stay married under those circumstances.

"No, but it was hard for them. Eventually they agreed with the decision I'd made. So having told them that, I thought it would be wise to wait a while before I told them I was gay." Katie laughed. "They wouldn't have been able to take two shocks in such a short space of time."

"I can see it would have been hard for them. But let's face it, parents should love their kids and that love should be unconditional. But telling them you're gay can try that. Especially after telling them you were no longer going to be married and would bring your child up without Bill."

"Your letters were like a breath of fresh air. You told me how sorry you were about our last morning together. Then you went on to try and explain how you felt. It was as if you were with me, talking to me. You write great letters."

"I try to write the way I talk."

"It works. I just needed time and my hormones were all over the place. Then time went on and you stopped. Why?"

"I didn't know if you were even reading them and if you weren't, you wouldn't reply. So if being together wasn't on the cards I needed to protect myself. I had a chat with Janey and Lucy.

They suggested I put a time limit on how long I was prepared to wait for you. I chose February, so you're cutting it fine," I said grinning. "I had to make sure I wasn't going to hurt too much. I could have ended up waiting forever if I hadn't put this time limit on it."

"Would you have really stuck to it?"

"No. Yeah, but I probably would've added on a few weeks just to make sure. Then I would have had to admit it was over." I squeezed Katie's hand.

"When you stopped writing, I thought I'd lost you. It was then that I decided I wanted to be with you. I knew I would have to tell my parents. How could I build a life, a family with you and lose the chance of involving my parents? That's when I told them about me. I knew I'd be taking a risk, but I wanted everything to be out in the open, even if it meant losing them. I just knew I couldn't live without you in my life. I couldn't go back to being the good Catholic daughter they wanted."

"How did they take it, did they accept it all right?"

"Dad didn't talk to me for a while, but Mum was fine. She said she could see I'd changed over the last year. She didn't think it was due to moving to New York with Bill. She never really liked Bill and maybe that's why she was able to accept what I was telling her. Dad eventually came round, especially when he nearly delivered Molly."

"Wow, how did that happen?"

"Molly decided she was going to make an early appearance. I was alone with Dad trying to make him understand. I so wanted him to be part of my life, part of his grandchild's life. I didn't want him to miss out. I'd been having slight pains off and on since I got up that morning, but I put it down to the curry I'd had the previous evening. Our conversation was quite heated and Dad was being quite intransigent. I couldn't believe he was being like that about his first grandchild. Then my water broke and I knew I should get to the hospital. Fortunately Dad put his feelings to one side to take me. As Molly was early Josie couldn't be my birthing partner so Dad stepped in. I know I couldn't believe it either." Katie had clocked my look. "I'd obviously been in what they call pre-labour and once the waters broke the pains became more intense and about seven hours later she was born. It was quite funny because even when Mum arrived Dad wouldn't give up his role as birthing partner. He was so proud to be watching his first grandchild making an appearance he forgot he wasn't talking to me," Katie said, remembering.

"How did you leave things?" I asked.

"Well, not all happy families, but all very civilised. Mum will come down to see us, but whether Dad will join her is another matter."

"Did you tell them about me?"

"Yes, I did. I wanted to make sure they knew everything, no more untruths. But don't worry, Dad won't be down insisting you make an honest woman of me." Katie laughed.

"Well, at least they're still talking to you. In time it will get better. With Molly around there's no way they're gonna cut you off."

"True."

Chapter Seventeen

WE SAT IN silence, each with our own thoughts. I knew I wanted to take Katie to bed and make love to her. However, I've never made love to a woman who'd recently given birth and I was worried whether it was too soon or not.

"I'm really tired after the drive. Can we go to bed?" Has she been taking lessons from Josie? Maybe they're mind reading sisters.

"Sure, do you want to take the guest room?" I gave Katie the choice, hoping she'd say no.

"No."

Yes, result!

"Okay you go on up, I'm sure you remember the way. I'll lock up and bring the baby listener with me."

Katie picked her bag up from the hall and went upstairs while I locked up and switched off the lights. Very domesticated, that's me. I picked up the baby listener and followed Katie up.

God, I was nervous. Yes, me, because it was going to be the first time we'd slept together. Well, we'd slept together before, but tonight sleep was the last thing I had on my mind, if you catch my drift?

I looked in on Molly. She was sleeping peacefully. I stood looking at her. She was so small and delicate, but she was beautiful.

Then I heard Katie come in.

"She looks so peaceful, doesn't she?" Katie asked as she stood behind me.

"Yeah, I guess you'll have to make the most of it. She'll soon be into everything," I said.

"True," Katie agreed.

Suddenly I felt the warmth of her body as she stepped closer. She was pressing herself against my back, her breasts against me. I crossed my arms over my chest. I was really nervous. This was what I wanted, yet I couldn't move. Katie took my arms, moved them to my sides and turned me to face her. The naked desire in her eyes was so obvious, calling me to her and I was lost in that desire. She kissed me so softly it felt like butterfly wings. Katie pulled back and looked at me. Her eyes held the question as her lips spoke the words.

"Are you okay?"

I couldn't speak, couldn't move.

"Jess?"

"God, Katie, you've no idea how okay I am," I managed to croak out through a tight throat. God, could I be more like a nervous schoolboy?

Katie looked at me and I saw a smile break out across those luscious, kissable lips. Finally I came to life and kissed her. Gently at first, then tentatively and nervously our tongues were dancing together to our own private tune.

Suddenly she pulled away.

"Not in front of Molly," she said, looking at her sleeping daughter.

I grinned, took her hand and led her to the bedroom. I closed the curtains, letting the landing light illuminate the room. I turned to Katie, who looked absolutely gorgeous, and wanted her so much.

I moved to her and pulled her to me. Our bodies fit together so well, but then they always had.

"Oh, Katie," I murmured against her lips as we kissed.

Kissing Katie was just as wonderful as I remembered. Only now it was even better because there was no worry about whether we should be doing it or not. It felt so right and it was so good. I felt myself getting more and more aroused. I was so wet and didn't know how long I could last.

I pulled away and looked at Katie. "Are you okay with this?"

Katie put her fingers against my lips.

I pulled Katie into my arms and kissed her again, my heart felt so full. The butterflies in my stomach were having one hell of a party. Katie responded and our bodies melted into each other. I wanted to touch and kiss every part of her and to taste her. I wanted to make her come until she screamed out my name.

I undressed her slowly, revelling in the joy of being able to do it. I no longer had to hold back. I looked at her and saw her eyes darken with arousal. She was almost devouring me with her desire. I removed her bra and cupped her breasts in my hands. I rubbed my palms over her nipples. Katie moaned as they hardened under my touch.

"God, you're so beautiful," I said.

I trailed kisses down her neck and over the pulse beating beneath her smooth skin. I took one of her hardened nipples into my mouth and played my tongue over it. Katie gasped. I stopped and looked at her. I was worried I'd been too rough.

"Please. Don't you dare stop," she said.

I needed no more encouragement. I gently lowered her to the bed and quickly undressed as she removed her panties. I couldn't wait to feel her naked body against mine. I looked at her lying there. She held her arms up as an invitation. I covered her body gently with mine and heard her sigh of pleasure. I knew then we were meant to be together. We kissed, our tongues exploring and tasting the warm moistness of our mouths. I settled in between her legs as I kissed her neck, down to her erect nipples. I took one in my mouth, gently played my tongue round it. I didn't think it could become any harder, but it did. Katie's breath was coming fast and her moans of pleasure increased. I held her nipple with my teeth and played my tongue over it. She was pushing her breast farther into my mouth and arching into me.

I looked up at her as she opened her eyes. They were almost black with desire and longing. I swear if I'd been a piece of paper I would have burst into flames with the look she gave me. It was the look she always gave me and it melted my heart. Katie was finally here in my arms and somehow I knew she was always going to be there.

"Jess, please. I can't wait. Oh, God, please?" Katie took my hand and put it between her thighs. I gasped as I found her soaking wet with desire.

"That's what you do to me."

God, she felt so good and any doubts I had were fading fast. All I could think of was how wet she was and how much pleasure I was giving her. She was certainly giving me plenty. I stroked her wetness, feeling her move with me, thrusting her hips into my hand. The folds of her skin, her erect engorged clitoris were all bathed with her juices. I entered her gently, smoothly and it felt so good. Wetness pooled between my legs and my clitoris pulsed. I didn't know how long I could last.

"Oh, Katie, my God you feel so good," I whispered against her mouth as I kissed her deeply.

My fingers were moving in and out, Katie's hips grinding up and down to my rhythm. We were dancing to the tune of our bodies and the love between us.

"Jess, oh, Jess. That. Feels. So. Good." Katie pushed her hips to take more of me.

"I want to taste you," I said, moving down. I was desperate to taste her.

"Yes, oh, Jess, yes."

I kissed down her stomach to her soft curls glistening wet in the gentle light. I could smell her arousal and couldn't wait to taste her. My tongue found her hard erect clitoris. I licked, teased and sucked it into my mouth. Katie moaned as she moved her hips into me and held my head. She needn't have worried as there was no way I was going to move now. She tasted so good and there was nothing more I wanted than to carry on drinking in her nectar. I wanted to give her pleasure. I licked and stroked her and pulled my fingers almost all the way out before plunging back in. I felt her open up to me each time I entered her. She pushed down to take more of me into her. I felt the gentle ripples as her orgasm began to build. It was nearly enough to tip me over the edge. She moaned and opened her legs. I went deeper. God I was enjoying this. I caught her hard clitoris with my teeth and I let my tongue continue its dance over the engorged tissue. Katie was so hard and she gasped as I gently tightened my teeth on her. I slowed then and just let my tongue rest on her. I wanted her to calm down then build slowly. I wanted her to scream out in pleasure.

"God, Jess, don't stop now. I need to come. Please."

I looked up at her face. Her eyes were pleading with me.

"Not yet baby, be patient."

I went back to her clitoris and gently licked the hard bud. Katie moaned. I licked and sucked it deep into my mouth and then entered her again with my fingers. She opened her legs farther, then I felt the ripples pulsating stronger against me. I curled my fingers to reach her G spot and pulled almost all the way out before plunging back in as she built up to her orgasm. I flicked her clitoris with my tongue and made long slow strokes up and down.

"Now, baby, now you can come."

She let go of my head and gripped the sheets as she shuddered and screamed out in ecstasy. I felt the shivers of the final throes of her orgasm. Slowly, her breathing came back to normal as her orgasm subsided. Just as she was coming down I started to lick and suck her again. My fingers continuing their deep slow in and out thrusts.

"Jess, I can't, not so soon," she said, but I felt her move into me. I needed no further encouragement. I increased my movements and Katie pushed farther to get more of me inside her.

"Yes you can. Come for me, baby."

I carried on licking and sucking on her clitoris and gently thrusting my fingers in and out, building up a gentle rhythm. Katie moved with me and almost immediately had a second orgasm, just as fierce as the first one. As she came back down I kissed my way languidly back up her body.

I lay in Katie's arms, where I'd wanted to be for so long. I heard her heart beating a rhythm that matched my own. I moved in closer and lazily stroked her breast and watched the rise and fall as she breathed. It felt so good in Katie's arms. I wanted to stay like this forever. "I didn't know I could do that," she said, breathlessly.

"You mean you've never had an orgasm before?"

"Of course, but my God, nothing like that, and never two on the trot. I guess I was never really interested in sex."

"Not interested in sex? That's not the impression I'm getting."

"I'm gonna give you more than an impression," Katie said, and kissed me. "Mmm not bad. If I taste this good you must taste even better."

She positioned herself on top of me and between my legs and kissed me deeply. Her hands finding my erect nipples as she did so. To be honest I didn't know how much I could take. I was so aroused after making love to Katie that I was ready to come the minute she touched me. My stomach quivered as her hand made its way to exactly where I wanted it. She found my wetness and gasped.

"This is the effect you have on me," I said.

"Oh, Jess, I love you so much." Katie kissed me as she whispered the words I'd longed to hear.

Her fingers moved into the wetness and found me hard and engorged. She caressed and stroked my clitoris. She slid two fingers inside me and I felt my orgasm building. Her fingers moved rhythmically and my hips moved in tune with them. God, it was so good to feel her inside me. I'd waited so long for this. I managed to control the urge to come. I wanted it to last. Wanted this first time to —

She stopped.

"Ha, playing my game, eh?" I asked breathlessly.

"No, I just want to taste you the way you tasted me." She moved down my body.

The anticipation! It was almost too much. I nearly came there and then.

"Oh, Katie, God I want you so much."

I felt her tongue touch my hard clitoris and I was in heaven. She licked and then pushed her tongue inside me, then a slow stroke back to my clitoris and circled it. She stroked up and down each side of it and I felt my orgasm building. I knew I was going to come harder than I'd ever done before. I was just thinking it couldn't get better when Katie surprised me by filling me with two fingers. I gasped and moaned and raised my hips into her. She thrust into me.

"Oh, yes, baby, harder. Oh God."

Katie responded by thrusting deeper and harder with long strokes of her beautiful fingers. Her tongue was working my clitoris, which was getting harder. I wanted to come, yet I wanted it to last forever. She increased her rhythm and that was it. I couldn't hold on any longer. It was just too much and I exploded. My orgasm came hard and strong. I felt my muscles tighten on Katie's fingers and I clamped Katie's head against me. I pushed up again and again to meet her mouth as my orgasm built and then slowly subsided. I fell back completely sated and I finally let Katie's head go.

"Sorry, I didn't mean to do that," I said.

"What? Have an orgasm?"

"No, holding your head like that, but I meant to have the orgasm," I said, as Katie moved up and lay her head on my shoulder.

"Was it — ?"

"It was." I was speechless.

"Was it really?" Katie sounded pleased with herself. "I was worried, as I've never made love with a woman before."

I laughed. "You have absolutely nothing to worry about."

She leaned over and kissed me.

She grinned. "I know I still have a lot to learn."

"Plenty of time for that. We've got all the time in the world to practice."

She curled up in my arms. It felt so good.

"Katie?"

"What?" She asked, quietly.

"I love you. I've probably loved you since the first time I met you."

"I know you do. I love you too," Katie said, sleepily.

I held her as her breathing slowed and I knew she was asleep. I was almost dropping off myself when I heard Molly on the baby alarm. Katie heard it too and started to get up.

"Leave her to me. I'm sure I can cope. Does she need feeding again?" I asked.

"No, she'll be fine until about two in the morning."

Oh, the joys of parenthood.

I got out of bed, put on my bathrobe and padded into the nursery. I never thought I'd have a nursery.

I went in and set the light to dim. Molly was wide-awake. I put the side of the cot down and picked her up. I still couldn't get over the fact of how light she was. I wrapped her in a blanket and sat in the rocker. I gently rocked, looking at Molly looking at me. I knew she couldn't actually see me, but it was nice the way she looked up at me. I was falling for her big time, which felt quite natural as she was Katie's daughter and I loved Katie very much.

"Do you know how lucky you are, Molly? You not only have one mummy, you have two. You also have a Dad who lives in New York, so you may not see him very often. But you should know that he loves you."

Molly wriggled. It was almost as if she understood everything I was saying.

"I love you too. You're so adorable, just like your mum. How could I not love you?"

I put my finger in her tiny hand and she gripped onto it. My throat constricted as I held back the tears that came unbidden to my eyes. It felt so good that she was holding onto me. I really did love this little bundle. I think I loved her as soon as Katie put her in my arms.

"I hope you're gonna be very happy living here. Well, I hope you're gonna be living here. I haven't actually asked your other mummy, but I will. I love your mummy so much and I never thought we'd get to this moment, but we have. Mind you I never thought I'd have a daughter, but I have."

I suddenly realised I thought of Molly as my daughter too. I just hoped Katie would agree to coming and living with me. I brought Molly up so her face touched my cheek. The smell of her was lovely, all baby-soap and powder. I kissed her cheek and settled her back in my arms again.

"I'm sure your mummy will agree to live here. I mean I've put a lot of work in, and you've got to admit your room is pretty cool. Of course, as you grow up, I'll have to change the décor. I don't suppose you'll always want Pooh Bear."

God, what have I let myself in for? I suddenly remembered my teenage years.

"I just hope you're not gonna be too much of a pain when you're a teenager."

I looked down into Molly's eyes and couldn't imagine her being an awful teenager. Mind you, only time would tell.

"You and me both. I can remember what I was like." Katie's voice made me jump.

"How long have you been there?" I asked, as I turned to look up at her. God, she was beautiful.

"Since you sat down with Molly."

"Didn't trust me not to drop her, eh?"

"No, nothing like that. I was going to get a drink when I heard you talking and I wanted to hear what you were saying."

"Well, if you heard it all, what's your answer?"

"Give her to me." Katie took Molly and then sat down on my lap.

Between us we cuddled each other and Molly. Could life get any better?

"Well?"

"Of course we'll move in with you. I want to spend the rest of my life with you. I love you so much."

I kissed Katie and then the top of Molly's head.

"How could I not want to live with the woman who loves my baby like her own?"

I looked down at Molly, now asleep in Katie's arms, and I knew all my Christmases had come at once.

The End

Other Yellow Rose Titles You Might Enjoy:

It'sElementary
by Jennifer Jackson

Tolerance and acceptance are growing in society, but don't tell that to a parent of a school-aged child. Teachers are supposed to be straight, wholesome, and good examples for the children they teach. This is why one vague rumor about a slightly effeminate teacher at Baxter Elementary resulted in a mob of angry parents demanding his removal. Victoria was a first hand witness to the carnage, which is why she vowed to never let her personal life mingle with her professional life. It was a good plan. That is until a most-certainly-not-her-type, absolutely adorable, first-year teacher got under her skin. And, when a confused and desperate parent targets her protégé, Victoria must decide which is more important: her career or love

ISBN 978-1-61929-084-6

Available in print and eBook formats

Strength In Numbers
by Jeanine Hoffman

Bailey ran out on her best friend, Jay, years ago but wants to make amends if she can. Sharon has buried herself in work for so long she isn't sure she knows how to do much else. Riley, a one-time LPGA golfer, has traveled and played the field while competing on some of the finest golf courses of the world. And, then there is Jay whose heart was broken by Bailey so many years ago - she hasn't fully trusted anyone since. All four women have things to face about themselves and the others. Fate brings them together to face a crisis none of them ever expected. Their lives will turn upside down, and the outcome can only be determined if they will believe that there is *Strength in Numbers*.

ISBN 978-1-61929-051-8

Available in print and eBook formats

The Chosen
by Verda Foster

In the feudal kingdom of Ryshta, there are masters and there are slaves. The servants labor for their arrogant lords, who treat them little better than animals. That's the way it's always been. But the slaves are waiting for the coming of The Chosen One, the prophesied leader who will take them out of their bondage.

A chance encounter separates Roslin, daughter of the king, from her privileged world. She takes refuge in a peasant community where she finds herself drawn to the charismatic Brice, leader of the slaves' rebellion. Is Brice indeed the Chosen?

The old order is eventually overturned and the slaves win their liberty. But in the new, free world, the unveiling of a carefully kept secret has as much impact on the ex-slaves as the rebellion had on their ex-masters. And Brice and Roslin have to face their own challenges as they explore their love for each other. A gripping story of love, battle and outstanding moral courage.

ISBN 978-1-61929-027-3

Available in print and eBook formats

Mountain Rescue: The Ascent
by Sky Croft

When your heart has been broken, can you ever trust again?

This is the question that Dr. Sydney Greenwood finds herself asking, when she relocates to a village in the Scottish Highlands, seeking a fresh start.

There, she joins the local Mountain Rescue team, and finds a new challenge in the form of Kelly Saber — an expert climber with a hidden past — who tests Sydney's resolve to stay single.

Amidst harsh terrain, turbulent weather, and life or death rescues, the two women must learn to trust each other, not only on the mountain, but in matters of the heart.

This is the first in the Mountain Rescue saga, how Saber and Sydney meet, the beginning of their relationship, and their first tests as a couple, both on and off the mountain. This is...The Ascent.

ISBN 978-1-61929-098

Available in print and eBook formats

Picking Up the Pieces
by Brenda Adcock

Athon Dailey hasn't had many breaks in her life other than the ones she made for herself by living up to her reputation as a tough girl until she meets Lauren Shelton, a new girl at school in Duvalle, Texas. Tamed by Lauren's affection, Athon begins to believe there could be a brighter future. When Lauren's parents discover the growing relationship they send her away, making sure the two girls never have contact, leaving Athon alone and abandoned.

Twenty years later the two women meet again. Athon has established a successful military career as a helicopter pilot while Lauren has returned to Duvalle to teach. It doesn't take long for them to rekindle their feelings for one another and they finally get the chance to rebuild their teenage dreams. Permanent happiness is within their grasp when Athon's unit is deployed.

Athon comes home in a coma, diagnosed with a traumatic brain injury. She awakens to find Lauren by her side to welcome her home. When Athon chooses to retire and return to Texas, neither realizes the twists and turns the journey home will take. The Athon Dailey who returned to Lauren is not the woman she remembers. In order for their relationship to survive, Lauren begins her search for the woman she loves. Will Athon finally find her way back to Lauren and the dream they both once had? Does Lauren have the courage to live with a woman who is now a stranger?

ISBN 978-1-61929-120-1

Available in print and eBook formats

Moving Target
by Melissa Good

Dar and Kerry both feel the cruise ship project seems off somehow, but they can't quite grasp what is wrong with the whole scenario. Things continue to go wrong and their competitors still look to be the culprits behind the problems. Then new information leads them to discover a plot that everyone finds difficult to believe. Out of her comfort zone yet again, Dar refuses to lose and launches a new plan that will be a win-win, only to find another major twist thrown in her path. With everyone believing Dar can somehow win the day, can Dar and Kerry pull off another miracle finish? Do they want to? □□Fans of this series should note that due to its length this story will be split into three novels. The determination of where to make that split was a joint decision between the author and the publisher. □□See the title Tropical Convergence for further details on the first part and the title Stormy Waters for details on the second part. □

ISBN 978-1-61929-150-8

Available in print and eBook formats

OTHER YELLOW ROSE PUBLICATIONS

Lori L. Lake	Different Dress	1-932300-08-2
Lori L. Lake	Ricochet In Time	1-932300-17-1
Lori L. Lake	Like Lovers Do	978-1-935053-66-8
K. E. Lane	And, Playing the Role of Herself	978-1-932300-72-7
Helen Macpherson	Love's Redemption	978-1-935053-04-0
J. Y Morgan	Learning To Trust	978-1-932300-59-8
J. Y. Morgan	Download	978-1-932300-88-8
A. K. Naten	Turning Tides	978-1-932300-47-5
Lynne Norris	One Promise	978-1-932300-92-5
Paula Offutt	Butch Girls Can Fix Anything	978-1-932300-74-1
Surtees and Dunne	True Colours	978-1-932300-529
Surtees and Dunne	Many Roads to Travel	978-1-932300-55-0
Vicki Stevenson	Family Affairs	978-1-932300-97-0
Vicki Stevenson	Family Values	978-1-932300-89-5
Vicki Stevenson	Family Ties	978-1-935053-03-3
Vicki Stevenson	Certain Personal Matters	978-1-935053-06-4
Vicki Stevenson	Callie's Dilemma	978-1-61929-003-7
Cate Swannell	A Long Time Coming	978-1-61929-062-4
Cate Swannell	Heart's Passage	978-1-932300-09-3
Cate Swannell	No Ocean Deep	978-1-932300-36-9

Be sure to check out our other imprints,
Quest Books, Mystic Books, Silver Dragon Books, Young Adult
Books, and Blue Beacon Books.

About the Author

Pauline George was born in the beautiful county of Kent and is the eldest of four children. She now lives halfway between the buzzing metropolis of London and the quiet countryside of the Surrey Hills. Writing has always been part of Pauline's life although most of it ended up on the cutting-room floor. Pauline indulges her hobbies of walking and photography when she isn't writing, and even whilst doing this, her mind is busy creating the stories she hopes you will enjoy reading.

VISIT US ONLINE AT
www.regalcrest.biz

At the Regal Crest Website You'll Find

- The latest news about forthcoming titles and new releases

- Our complete backlist of romance, mystery, thriller and adventure titles

- Information about your favorite authors

- Current bestsellers

- Media tearsheets to print and take with you when you shop

- Which books are also available as eBooks.

Regal Crest print titles are available from all progressive booksellers including numerous sources online. Our distributors are Bella Distribution and Ingram.

CPSIA information can be obtained at www.ICGtesting.com
Printed in the USA
LVOW08s2213280214

375554LV00004B/810/P